The Importance of Manners

a novel

H.G.Watt

First published 2015

Freight Books
49-53 Virginia Street
Glasgow, G1 1TS
www.freightbooks.co.uk

A CIP catalogue reference for this book is available from the British Library.

ISBN 978-1-910449-20-2
eISBN 978-1-910449-21-9

Typeset by Freight
Printed and bound by Bell and Bain, Glasgow

the publisher acknowledges investment from
Creative Scotland toward the publication of this book

For my husband, who saved me from
falling into a pit of pythons.

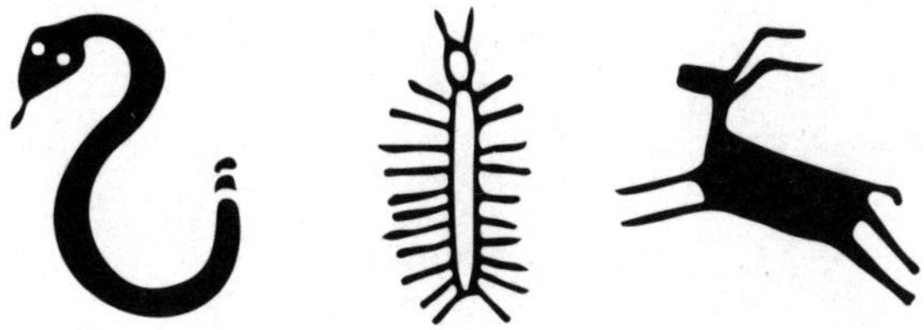

Burt Darwin's Journal

On his eighteenth day at sea, Burt Darwin leaned over a long railing, his red nose peeling unattractively.

From here the African continent looks like any other, he wrote in inelegant script. *A thin brown-yellow strip on the horizon. The ocean is more interesting.*

If Burt Darwin had been an observant man he might have noticed the opulent orange of the sand dunes just across the water, or the plum-purple shadows that fell beneath them. He might have exclaimed at the beauty of the navy sky or felt the heat of the land as it hummed with the beating of mosquito wings. He might have felt the pulse that was, and could only belong to, Africa.

But he didn't.

Burt Darwin saw what he saw and wrote dutifully in his hand-stitched and leather bound journal, the most precious of the items he carted around in his cheap valise.

'It will bring you great riches,' he had been told when he found it amongst a stack of rolled up love spells in a witchcraft store in Northampton, Massachusetts. 'It is the oldest kind of magic. Just fill each page with Truth and you'll be the richest man in the world.' This quaint and practiced speech was made by the owner of the store. A self-proclaimed Wiccan, he moved about with an unbalanced shuffle, swinging his wooden leg out in front of him, and then following it with the rest of his bulk. Once, a regular customer had asked why he did not use a modern prosthetic leg.

'Something out of silicon and metal and stuff,' the customer said.

The Wiccan took great offense at this question. 'How then, would anyone recognise me?' he replied with a sneer. And so the Wiccan shuffled and shifted awkwardly, finding the perfect crooked angle to simultaneously stay on his foot and bend over Burt Darwin's shoulder.

'It is the oldest kind of magic. Just fill each page with Truth and you'll be the richest man in the world.'

'I do not care much for money,' Burt Darwin replied.

'Then you do care a little, and a little is enough!' proclaimed the Wiccan.

Unconvinced, Burt Darwin moved on to the next aisle where boxes of colourful candles were marked with little brown tags.

Love, Fear, Hate, Revenge.

'Do you have any candles for the afterlife?' Burt Darwin asked.

'The afterlife?' The Wiccan shuffled quickly, his arms flying about like a tightrope walker making a big show of losing his balance. 'No, no candles for the afterlife. But this journal is the perfect thing! After all, if you have no riches in this life, then you will be a poor man in the next place too!'

One of Burt Darwin's large hooded eyes narrowed as curious afternoon light dove through hanging crystals and projected rainbows on his bald patch.

'How do you know that?' he asked, his voice serious and low. It just so happened that Burt Darwin was a man who lived for the afterlife.

'Ah, but just think of Egypt!' The Wiccan pointed out the door. Burt Darwin followed his finger, half expecting to see a dark woman in a white tunic and golden headdress. 'The Pharaohs were buried with their riches and even their slaves in preparation for the next life. They knew what they were about!'

Burt Darwin fished for his wallet, sifted through bits of paper and old receipts until he found $12.99 in dollar bills, quarters and copper cents. Pleased with his purchase, he began the long process of filling his money-making-journal with Truth.

From here the African continent looks like any other. A thin brown-yellow strip on the horizon. The ocean is more interesting. A group of flying fish jumped out of the water. I counted eight of them. They were silver and black and flew over the waves for several seconds before disappearing back into the blue.

The boat rocked softly from side to side, the temperature cooling to a less uncomfortably warm degree as land moved out of sight. Burt Darwin shifted his stance, moving his sock and sandal-encased feet wider apart to keep his balance. Turning to a new page in his precious journal he wrote:

The floors on this deck are sickly white and the varnish along the wooden railing is shiny and looks sticky. I hesitated before touching it earlier. I don't like stickiness. I also don't like April, it is the dullest month. But it's finished, nearly finished. Tomorrow it will be over.

Burt Darwin stopped writing, the tip of his white plastic pen raised and pointing at the pink-streaked sky. He was an easily distracted man, and this time his attention had wandered to a passing guest who could not have been described as pretty by any stretch of the imagination. She was the kind of woman who commanded attention through her sheer largeness.

Large feet covered in large stockings falling down even larger thighs beneath large skirts billowing under the shadow of a large chest and monstrous hat. But it was none of these things that drew Burt Darwin's eye. Nor was it the woman's long plastic eyelashes or her purple painted lips. It was something far smaller: a sparkling pendant squished in a pit of sweat between her massive breasts.

'Excuse me miss,' he said, in his smooth southern accent.

'Yes?' The woman stopped. She looked at him

with tempered distaste – a result of the favourable accent – and waited for the forthcoming explanation. Later that evening at dinner, she would tell the tale of the encounter and say it was Burt Darwin's accent that almost pardoned him his too large nose, oily mustache and bony legs. She would also claim that she caught him looking at her breasts, because she wanted the couples at her table to believe she had been desired. Being wanted, even by an ugly man, would have made her happy.

'I wonder, that charm you are wearing, is it local?' Burt Darwin asked.

'This old thing? Oh, no. I bought it in India a few years ago. It's an "Om" sign, made from rubies of course.'

Recognising the Hindu symbol, Burt Darwin pulled seven strings from under his Hawaiian patterned shirt and found an Om amongst the dozens of other charms he wore around his neck. The sound was the manifestation of the divine, the unification of Bhrahma, Vishnu and Shiva: creation, preservation, destruction. When he was Hindu, Burt Darwin was a follower of Vishnu who could give moksha, and liberate followers from the cycle of rebirths. But he was not Hindu just then.

'Why did you ask?' The large one wanted to know.

Burt Darwin may have responded but, distracted by the sight of his white plastic pen, his mind skipped from *white* to *shirt* to *underwear.* Remembering that he had meant to go downstairs and check if his laundry had been delivered to his stateroom, he left the confused woman's side.

On his way to his room, Burt Darwin would get distracted several more times. First by the painting of a polar bear hanging beside the door of the Narcissus Spa, then by the sound of coins falling into metal containers at the casino and finally by the captain's voice as he spoke over the intercom:

Good afternoon ladies and gentlemen, this is your master and commander speaking from the bridge. We are proceeding very nicely on course to Cotonou, Benin, and your Beautiful White Lady should reach port by 6am tomorrow morning...

The Beautiful White Lady

The Grand Mariner was not an extraordinarily big vessel, and some of its passengers, like Lady Chanel Malory, thought it too small. Chanel had harboured grander hopes for the ship and was disappointed by almost every one of the eleven decks.

The Narcissus Spa on deck nine offered manicures and pedicures, but did not carry her favourite shade of nail polish. They had "Cherry Red", "Orchid White", "Peachy Peach", "Plum Purple" and "Raspberry Pink" that one could purchase for $16.99 a bottle, but there wasn't any silver varnish in sight. Silver varnish made Chanel think of silver-lined mirrors, which in turn reminded her of the silver-backed brush her mother had inherited from a distant relative that drowned in the Starnbergersee.

The casino on deck five had twenty-five slot machines, two poker tables and two black jack tables. This should have satisfied a woman such as Chanel since she did not gamble as a rule (she preferred to act the part of lucky charm), but the bar upset her deeply. Instead of serving shaken martinis to handsome men in tuxedos, the bartenders dished out cosmopolitans and piña coladas to ladies with wrinkled hands and white hair.

But it was the library on deck ten which disappointed her most of all. Stocked full of travel books, biographies and novels that had become "classics" (a word which, to Chanel's mind, was synonymous with "unreadable"), none of the six large bookshelves carried a single romance. And romance was what she lived for.

The Tahitian Lounge on deck eleven was Chanel's only source of solace, and that was where she could be found on afternoons such as these. Amongst the plotted plants, teak chairs and multi-coloured cushions with their amorphous shapes that looked somewhere between leaves and curled up naked men with pot-bellies, Chanel sat with one ankle crossed over the other. From under the shadow of her jaunty sun hat she waited as her favourite waiter served her a weak cup of tea. He called her Ma'am, as he did every day, with what she mistakenly believed to be an Australian accent.

'Merci,' Chanel simpered, her eyes cast down the way she had seen Vivienne Leigh do in *Gone With the Wind.* Her fake Australian bowed before turning to afford her with a nice view of his backside. He had what she would call a Tony Little bum.

'It says here that you are not to wear any jewelry when we disembark in Benin.'

Chanel raised an eyebrow as she turned to her husband.

Lord Percival Mallory, known as Percy to his Cambridge chums, had his face buried in the daily cruise paper. He turned the page, rattling the sheets as he would have with his beloved *Times,* and was left highly dissatisfied with the meagre crackle the glossy paper made.

'I am not taking off my wedding ring!' Chanel said firmly.

She held up her hand to admire the huge glittering diamond. The rock had been in Percy's family for generations and made Chanel the envy of all British socialites. No matter how much they whispered about the *"French* interloper", none of them could say that "The Eye of the Tiger" would look better on anyone else's finger. After all, before marrying Percy, Chanel had been a famous hand model. Her hand had graced the pages of *Elle, Marie Claire* and even *Horse and Hound.*

'It says here that the average income in Benin is $1 a day,' Percy continued in his ever-dry tone. 'And that you should leave diamonds and gold on the ship if you want to keep your fingers and earlobes.'

'Really?' Chanel reached for the paper, forgetting that Percival Mallory hated nothing more than to have something, anything at all, taken from him.

'Now now Chanel, control yourself! I have forgiven your love of snails, coffee and romance. I am even willing to look past your surrender-monkey heritage as I have so often told you, but I will not condone any grabbing!'

It was in moments like these that Chanel Mallory, born Jana Kreitmeir in Dortmund, Germany (about 200 miles from the French border) felt a twinge of sympathy for her clueless husband. For as much as Percy loved to read his precious newspaper and those tedious classics, he knew so little about life. After all, everyone of any intelligence knew that the French had never been mistaken for monkeys. Chanel assumed that he had to be thinking of the Japanese, but she would not say as much. Watching her old husband behave foolishly made her feel like Jane Eyre.

'You are right, Percy. I am sorry.'

Percy snorted.

'Oh listen, listen! The band out by the pool is playing the theme song from Titanic! That was just the most romantic movie, non?'

'Not one copy of the *Times* and they call this a luxury cruise!' Percy grumbled. 'I think it's time to write a sternly worded letter!'

Swept away by the romance of it all, Chanel made a half-hearted attempt to drag her husband to the poolside, then set off on her own, leaving him to his letter writing.

Had the loiterers around the dance floor known that Chanel would save the world before the next day was through, they may have been kinder in their thoughts. Or at least in their whispers. But no one knew what was to come. They only saw what they saw; a South African waiter called Jack offering to show Chanel the lower decks of the ship, and her agreeing on the condition that he would call her Rose.

Roses Are Red, But Not Always

Ever since he had begun writing in his journal, Burt Darwin had become increasingly aware of the prevalence of lies. They were everywhere one looked, and the onboard shop of the Grande Mariner was no exception. Stepping through the glass doors, Burt Darwin took note of the row of shampoos on a shelf to his right. To his left were dozens of bottles of suntan lotion, a few packs of AA batteries and only one leftover pack of dental floss (a sure sign that Americans were onboard).

His eyes travelled over the multitude of claims written in large bold fonts across the store:

100% Relief, 24hour Protection, The Best, The Only, The Strongest, The Newest, The Longest Lasting... lies, all of them. And perhaps the funniest thing of all was that people accepted being lied to as a natural thing. No one really believed that the shampoo they were buying was really THE WORLD'S BEST SHAMPOO. No one really believed that ginger tablets CURE SEASICKNESS IN A HEARTBEAT. But they bought the products anyway, hoping that they did at least a bit of what they claimed to do.

Grabbing a pack of gum that promised to refresh him (if anything the gum would stimulate his stomach acids and make him feel hungry), Burt Darwin ambled over to the till where an Asian crew member was busily punching keys on the register.

'Would you like me to put this in a bag for you?' the cashier asked the woman waiting patiently across from her.

'No thank you dear,' came the reply. 'Our Lord told us not to be wasteful.'

The Asian cashier looked none the wiser, but handed over the family sized pack of toffee popcorn without comment.

'Which Lord?' Burt Darwin wanted to know.

The customer blinked at him with surprise.

'Why our Lord and saviour, Jesus Christ of course.' Now that the woman had turned his way, Burt Darwin noticed that she was dressed like Mother Teresa. Complete with the blue striped white robes and worn nun sandals, if she had the hat-veil thing she could have been Mother Teresa's sister, or at least her twice-removed cousin.

'Are you a nun?' he asked.

'I will be one day,' the woman smiled as she touched the silver-coated cross around her neck. 'My name is Sister Mary.'

Burt Darwin couldn't recall if women carried the title "sister" before they became nuns, but that was neither here nor there. He was not a man that judged religious practices, he merely collected them.

'So Jesus said not to use plastic bags?' Burt Darwin asked as he opened his journal to a fresh page and pulled a plastic pen from his pocket.

'If he had lived to see this day, he would have,' Sister Mary assured him.

Burt Darwin wrote quickly.

'What about dental floss?' Stalling his scribbles to look at the baffled Sister's face, he tried again. 'Would Jesus approve of flossing?'

'Flossing? No. Flossing is blasphemous.'

The woman with the massive breasts has three short hairs coming out of the mole on her chin. She says flossing is blasphemy.

'I am off to pray for the souls of sinners. Would you care to join me?' Sister Mary asked.

'I only pray for my own soul,' Burt Darwin said before putting his pen back into his pocket and walking out of the store.

Sister Mary blinked twice, reached for the tester of a Calvin Klein perfume sitting on a nearby shelf, then changed her mind. It would not do to wear perfume and attract the lust of men. Although she really did like that particular scent, it was just sweet enough and just floral enough to please her.

It was difficult to be a woman of faith.

She browsed through the photographs along the wall beside the shop. The ship's photographer, Antoine, had printed out the pictures from the previous evening's formal dinner and there were still some disembarkation photos from Luderitz. Tearing open the corner of her bag of toffee popcorn, Sister Mary chewed noisily on the sickly sweet morsels as she admired some of the jewellery passengers had been wearing.

A massive yellow diamond on a skinny blonde

with disproportionately large boobs held her attention for a moment longer than the rest.

'Definitely fake,' she said to no one in particular.

Eighteen bits of popcorn later, Sister Mary moved on past the Crooners Lounge before reaching the Casino. The slot machines were making their customary noises: *Ding-Ding-Ding-Ding. Ka-ching.* Nobody noticed the sounds were coming from the only machine that was unoccupied. Those that had people sitting in front of them only gave off silence and a random, fart-like "Beep" once every so often.

Nevertheless, the casino was anything but quiet. Amongst the sporadic beeps and the misleading *Ka-Chings* were the uproarious voices of those that sat at the tables. Sister Mary found a seat at a slot machine near the Black Jack table where a balding man slapped his hand on the green and yelled, 'Give me another!'

It took a moment for the croupier to decide if the customer was asking for another card or if he wanted another drink.

'Another Long Island Ice Tea coming right up sir,' a waitress smiled politely as she moved away to the bar.

The man frowned at the croupier, 'Come on man, another card!'

Sister Mary chucked another toffee-covered popped piece of corn in her mouth, watched the balding man go bust, put her hands together and began to pray:

Dear Lord, please give the balding man at the Black Jack table strength for he knows not what he does. Everyone in their right mind would have stayed at 18, especially when the house was showing a weak 4. Please clear his vision and help him see the error of his ways.

Burnt Food

'Good evening, I trust you are all enjoying your dinner?'

'Oui, merci.' Chanel puckered her lips at the thirty-year old man with the white blazer who approached their table.

'Who are you?' Percy asked, thoroughly annoyed. He hated the very American tradition of bothering people during a meal. Even if he had been enjoying his food, the vulgar interruption by the yellowish-skinned waiter had definitely ruined it for him.

'My name is Carlos. I am the Food and Beverage Manager! I introduce myself when you first arrived!'

'I am meant to remember that, am I?' Percy

muttered.

'I remember,' Chanel said quickly, moving her arm so the strap of her red Gucci dress slipped down her shoulder a notch. Carlos watched with enthusiasm and leaned an arm on the back of her chair.

'Well since you are here, you might as well take this plate away and tell whoever it is back there that calls himself a chef that he should replace the word *roasted* with *burned* on the menu,' Percy said, pushing his plate away.

'You are unsatisfied with the food señor?' Carlos asked, noticing the couple at the next table straining to hear what was being said. 'I assure you there must be some mistake. Our chefs are some of the best in the world!'

'The mistake is expecting decent fare from an Australian cook!' Percy thundered.

Carlos forced a smile as he signaled for a nearby waiter to approach. It was not his job to pick up plates and he would make no exception for the English man who dared to judge the restaurants' food. What could a Brit know about food? What culinary delights did they have to offer the world? Fish and chips? Pies? Carlos had been to England on many occasions and found the best food to be had was in the Indian restaurants.

'Take the gentleman's plate away,' he ordered, as a white gloved waiter approached.

Chanel batted her eyelashes. 'I like my food.'

'Of course you do, my dear,' Percy smiled at his wife. 'I am sure vomiting vile food makes you feel less guilty than wasting a perfectly good meal.'

'I used to be a model,' Chanel explained. In her head, "model" and "bulimia" were synonyms.

Carlos's lips had twisted in a semblance of a smile. He couldn't care less about the grotesquely rich couple's eating habits, he was interested only in his tip. The arrival of an Asian couple drew his attention. Asians were far better tippers than stuffy Brits. 'I must take my leave. I trust you will enjoy the dessert sir. It is a delicacy from my home town in Portugal.'

The couple from the adjacent table leaned over as the Food and Beverage Manager moved away.

'I thought he was I-talian.' The woman raised an eyebrow, looking from her husband to Percy as the Queen's English rolled off her tongue with the sort of haughtiness that public school pupils work for years to master.

'What difference does it make, dear?' her husband wanted to know.

'Quite right,' Percy agreed. 'They are all bloody foreigners.'

'But Percy, *I* am a foreigner.' Chanel said.

'Exactly. And lucky you are too. I wouldn't have forgiven a proper person the *grabbing* you were doing earlier.'

Two gasps were uttered in perfect unison at the neighbouring table.

'Grabbing. How very savage!'

'No one understands the importance of manners anymore.'

Chanel stared the fish-faced couple down, her bejeweled hand raised to her chin and the rock pointing at their gill-less heads The unattractive couple, already suffering from bad skin and over-long toes, withered under the aesthetic force, but tried to rally with strategic shifting that drew attention to the matching Valentino scarves hanging off the backs of their chairs. A quick tilt of the neck and the diamond studs in Chanel's ears caught the glint off the main dining room's many crystal chandeliers. The couple swallowed hard, the wife peeping the toe of her Dior pumps from under the long white table cloth for one last attempt at balance.

There was no balance to be had. The boat tipped ever so slightly, bowing to the splendour of the six-inch Pradas gracing the feet of the woman who had come out victorious.

Chanel lowered her hand, 'Better to live among savages and goat-herds, zan with sparkly, ugly-lipstick-wearing toffs!'

Percy's eyes widened, his nose flared, his brow twitched, his fingers curled and his lips moved as if to speak, but the sudden lightbulb that went off in his head stalled him into muteness. Only one other was silent in the overcrowded assembly of carnivores.

Six tables over, Burt Darwin recalled the instructions in The Book of Shadows as he finished slicing a banana. He had become a Wiccan two minutes before a waiter asked him for his order, and was now arranging his plate accordingly. With the three interlocked spirals of his triskelion pendant hanging over his shirt, he pushed slices of the yellow fruit to the left side of his plate.

Ruled by mars, the banana would prevent harm from coming to him as he travelled. The apple on the right side of his plate was the sacred fruit of the goddess; good for immortality. The bacon in the center was ruled by Adonis, which would help increase his earnings. The Mercury food, spaghetti, was at the bottom of the plate. While it would normally give him protection, Burt Darwin would not touch it just yet. In a few minutes he would be a Pastafarian and worship the farfalle.

Drawing a pentagram over his food with the bottle of Ketchup he had requested, Burt Darwin opened Gerald Gardener's *High Magic's Aid* and recited the Eko Eko Chant:

Eko, eko, Zomelak
Bazabi lacha bachabe
Lamac cahi achababe
Karrellyos
Lamac lamac Bachalyas
Cabahagy sabalyos
Baryolos
Lagoz atha cabyolas
Samahac atha famolas
Hurrahya!

Forks and knives were released and glasses put down as three chimes sounded to indicate the captain was about to speak over the intercom.

Within seconds the crowded dining room had gone silent.

Good evening ladies and gentlemen, this is your master and commander speaking from the bridge. I hope you are all enjoying your dinner, I do not wish to keep you from it for too long. This announcement is to notify you of rising swells and the probability of a gentle rocking throughout the ship. Please hang on to the railings as you walk up and down the stairs and remember you have no reason to be concerned. Your Beautiful White Lady is perfectly safe and will carry you with ease to our next port which is Cotonou…

A Gentle Rocking

Sister Mary reminded herself that many who had given their lives to spread the Lord's word had met with great challenges along the way. Then she ran for the railing and hurled her roasted beef dinner over the edge of the Grand Mariner.

'Are you alright?' A crew member appeared beside her shoulder. She was a young blonde, the kind that stirred men's passions without an ounce of effort.

'I am suffering as our Lord suffered on the path of righteousness. You should consider doing the same, dear.' Sister Mary raised her voice to be heard over the blazing wind. A large chunk of mutilated cow, covered in something greenish that had clung to her chin, chose that moment to fly and land on the crew member's neck.

'That's better,' Sister Mary patted the girl's back as the blonde gripped the bars and thrust her head over the railing. 'A little suffering goes a long way to make people better human beings. It will make you less of a harlot too.'

She left the puking girl's side, her rosary firmly in hand, and went back inside deck eleven. Seeing the sign for the Tahitian Lounge, Sister Mary followed with the trained instincts of one who has sought out sinners for many years.

The Lounge was unusually crowded for this time of night. People sat in groups of two, four and six as if afraid that chairs grouped in an odd number would make the world implode or worse, bring bad luck. Sister Mary found an empty seat at the bar and sat, her fingers itching.

'Excuse me, can I get some nuts please?' she asked the bartender.

'Certainly Madame.' The young man winked at her before turning to get her nuts. Sister Mary watched him move around the long bar area as a voice came over the microphone.

'And our last late night trivia question of the day: Who is the Greek God of the Underworld?' Sister Mary crossed herself. A hand flew up in excitement.

'I know!' Chanel beamed, to the accompaniment of several snorts.

'You are meant to write the answer down,' Burt Darwin said quietly. He looked out the window ignoring his blank quiz sheet and the stubby yellow pencil that rolled from one side of the table to the other before finally landing on the floor. He turned to a new page in his journal:

It is so dark outside that only the white foam of the waves can be seen, and that only when they come close enough to reflect the lights from the ship. The woman at the next table is saying that she counted twenty-seven doors with Do Not Disturb signs on her way up to the lounge. The woman is also saying that she supposes people are lying down in an effort to quell the nausea. Her suppositions are ridiculous. There are hundreds of possible scenarios for what is happening inside those doors.

'Did you see this?' Percy asked of no one in particular. Burt Darwin continued to write and the grandpa beside him continued to snore softly. Only Chanel, who had finished scribbling the wrong answer on her quiz paper, paid attention.

'See what?'

Percy shook the paper in his hand.

'The only newspaper on the entire ship and it's an Israeli one!' He threw the broadsheet on the table.

Chanel picked up the paper, her eyes skimmed over the bold headlines, passing disinterestedly over death, murder and war until she smiled, 'Oh but look! It's a joke! I love jokes!'

The woman in the pink sequin dress likes jokes.

'A Russian Jew's son was called to serve in ze Czar's army against ze Ottoman Turks,' Chanel translated slowly. 'Ze mother said to her son, "Don't over exert yourself! Just Kill a Turk and zen rest. Kill another Turk, zen rest again". Her son replied, "But mother, what if ze Turk kills me?" "Kill you?" exclaimed his mother. "But why? What have you done to him?"'

Chanel finished the joke with a little giggle. It wasn't that she found the joke particularly funny, but it seemed wrong not to laugh.

The old man beside me has stopped snoring. He looks dead.

'Since when can you read Israeli?' Percy wanted to know.

Chanel put the paper down. Every Jew knew

Hebrew. What an outrageous question! 'Wouldn't it be romantic to meet ze God of ze Underworld?' she said suddenly.

'Hardly,' Burt Darwin replied, having given the matter much thought. He played with one of the many rings he wore. This particular one was on his left pointing finger, and had a crystalline white powder in its hollow centre.

Thinking of killing yourself again? came a voice from the ether.

'I wouldn't bother trying to talk sense with her.' Percy picked up the paper, then got angry once more. 'Nothing in the bloody pages makes sense. Just write properly already! And what is with that awful font?'

Late At Night

Under the watchful eye of Scorpius and the whipping path of Orion's belt, the Beautiful White Lady sloshed through the Atlantic waters. Darkness pressed against the vessel with slippery hands, the lights pointing outwards from the lowest deck turning the water beneath them green. Through the green-black eeriness the ship moved, carrying hundreds of passengers, each one more foreign than the next. They were all alien to this part of the earth. Gill-less, fin-less, flipper-less, these mammals did not belong, and the howling wind told them so.

It crept through deck doors that had been left ajar and the nearly invisible holes left by gluttonous termites. It peeked into the dark library, rushed through silent slot machines and crossed into the long empty corridors. Carrying the scent of disinfectant carpet spray across the dimly lit hallways, the wind found room 4806 and knocked twice before running away.

Burt Darwin stirred in his uncomfortable bed, his eyes fluttering open, then fixing on the fire alarm above his head. A quick look out the tiny window to his right confirmed that he should be asleep still. Sitting up, he swung his feet off the side of the cot and wiggled his hairy toes.

'Well, since I'm up…' Burt Darwin spoke as he heaved himself off the mattress. He liked to speak as soon as he woke, just to erase the possibility that he had died in his sleep and had woken a spirit. Everyone knew spirits could not speak.

Now you are just being a dumb-ass.

He crossed quickly to the prayer rug in the corner of his room and aligned his heels with the back edge of the material. The Star of David, the wooden cross and the statue of Buddha at the top end of the rectangular carpet were barely visible in the darkness of the room, but Burt Darwin knew where they were and saluted them one by one. Then, lifting his arms high above his head, he breathed in deeply and bent to touch his toes.

And there you go with those monkey stretches again. I've told you a million times you aren't going to lose any weight without cardio...

As Burt Darwin performed his salutation to the night, he murmured Islamic prayers intermitted with Hindu chants and hand gestures that resembled parts of a Tai Chi sequence. These murmurings and movements were oddly in sync with the grunts coming from the bedroom two decks below.

'That was amazing,' the blackjack dealer said as he rolled sideways and dragged the sheets to cover his rapidly shrinking manhood.

Chanel tugged the material back and watched the rather unimpressive cock of her companion shrivel. It was a disgusting sight really, much like the pockmarked features of the man beside her. The whole experience had been sordid, which was just perfect.

'Lady Mallory...'

'I asked you to call me Evita,' Chanel chided.

The blackjack dealer looked disgruntled for a split second, then he shrugged. He'd had his fun with the rich crazy woman, and now it was time to get rid of her. 'Evita, I have a seven o'clock shift...'

Chanel was not stupid. She knew very well that they were only a few hours from port, and the casino would be closed for the entire day as per international maritime laws. But she smiled brightly anyway, looking inordinately pleased to be shooed in such a callous manner. And indeed she was.

Slipping into her red dress, she took a Prada stiletto in each hand and left her dealer's cabin. Laughter rose behind several closed doors as she made her way past lowly crew accommodation. There was no one to be seen, but evidence of a hallway party was strewn across the worn carpet. Avoiding beer cans, some non-descript yellow mush and a single abandoned life-vest, Chanel reached the bottom of the staircase and smiled at the cold-wet feeling beneath her French-manicured toes. Having stepped into spilled sauce, she trailed partial red-footprints up three sets of staircases before walking out into the whipping night air.

Then, abandoning her shoes, she gripped the slippery railing of the Beautiful White Lady, closed her eyes and sang: *Don't cry for me Argentina…*

Her voice travelled over Hokusai waves, sleeping sharks and hungry algae before it reached the lone man. The pirate stood with legs akimbo as his small land cruiser rocked perilously in the giant shadow of the cruise ship. Behind him, a wooden case full of M60's rolled from side to side as his walky-talky sputtered to life.

'No go,' came the voice from the small rectangle.

'Why the fuck not?' the pirate wanted to know.

'Number 11684 foresees problems. Will see you back at rendezvous point in 2 days. Out.' The crackle disappeared as the line went dead.

The pirate cursed. They had been planning this heist for months and tonight was meant to be his night, his coup de grace. He had worked in dozens of crews, hijacked a Greek oil tanker, attacked a Luxembourgish anchor handling vessel, boarded a UK-flagged cargo ship but this – this was different. Tonight's plan would have made them the first pirates in the Gulf of Guinea to attack a cruise ship.

What could have gone wrong? They had five guys on board the Grand Mariner, everyone was paid off at the ministry, the coast guards were looking the other way and the boats were in position. He could see them from where he stood, tiny jet-black spots on the onyx water. And between them their target – a floating palace of riches. Passengers with stacks of cash and no weapons. The Casino safe with hundreds and thousands in neatly stacked piles. The ship stores loaded with rolexes, and blood diamonds claiming to be clean.

Dirty fuckers, all of them. Floating by on a boat that had enough shit to feed, clothe and raise every poor kid in his country. They deserved to be robbed. They deserved a lot worse.

Hacking up a lump of phlegm, he spat it over the side of the boat. His fingers itched. His eyes focused on the back of the disappearing cruise ship. Slipping his fingers into the top pocket of his army grade bullet proof vest, he pulled out some khat and chewed.

Euphoria was a living thing.

Fuck this cruise ship. He would pillage the next one.

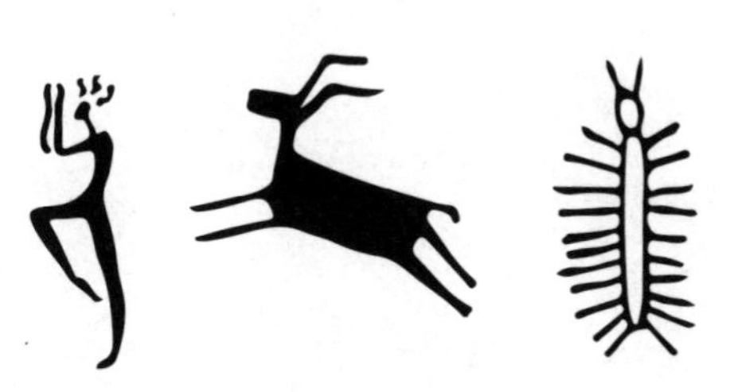

A Buzz Buzzing

The malaria-ridden mosquito buzzed, tired from its seemingly endless journey from the shore to the breakfast terrace of the docked cruise ship. Early morning was an odd time of day for her ilk, who considered dusk prime hunting hour, but today was a special day. Today was the day for breaking all the rules on the quest for mosquito El Dorado; a fat, European diabetic.

Honing in on the waft of carbon dioxide, the world's deadliest animal continued bravely on its mission, while the clueless inhabitants of the Grande Mariner filled their plates. Despite the earliness of the hour, nearly all the tables on the terrace were occupied. And of the three chairs that appeared empty, two had pool towels thrown across them. A few novice travelers looked at these towels and couldn't make sense of it, but the veterans onboard recognized the international sign of the German tourist with ease. These same seasoned conquistadors knew that in this floating melting pot of culture, humanity became easier to classify and categorize. Here at the Beautiful White Lady's breakfast buffet, homo sapiens uncoiled, becoming readable to even a tiny mosquito.

Yellow towers of syrup-coloured spheres, whisked shades of orange, and yolk fried in reused, fat-lined the freshly sterilized tables. Burned, stirred, flipped, slapped and consumed with slabs of fresh fat, cubed fat, thickened and creamed fat, the spread was the breakfast of champions. And it was amongst this cacophony of scents and click-clicking of aged jaws, that the mosquito landed on a white couple's table.

'Oh my God, look at that woman!'

'Which woman?' The husband turned quickly, trying to locate a female that may have attracted his wife's attention. There was a fat woman in what looked like a nun outfit carrying a plate of food drenched in chocolate sauce. No, she couldn't be the one. His wife was portly herself, and self-conscious about what she considered her only imperfection; the look of smirky horror couldn't be about a woman's fatness.

A few paces away, a white-haired granny had dropped her teeth and was following the precious accessory as it got kicked about by uncaring feet. No. That couldn't spur humour in his sensitive wife whose obsession with planning ensured her left eye, her aged eye, was always on the lookout for her own white-haired self.

'You mean the blonde?' he asked, thinking the young bride of the old Englishman with the awful taste in suits, might have caused that gleam of disdain. He had seen the couple many times before. The woman was hard to miss, especially today with that white dress…

'What blonde?'

'I mean the brunette,' he corrected quickly, hoping to stall the series of events that always followed that particular tone. *What blonde.* It seemed an innocent enough question, but what it actually meant was clear to him: *A blonde? Is she attractive? You find her attractive don't you? You must do, since you noticed her. She is more attractive than me, isn't she? You haven't found me attractive since our second baby popped out and destroyed any chance I had at regaining my figure. It's true isn't it? You think I'm ugly now. You are repulsed by the pouch of fat tucked just inside my waist band and my neck. Oh god, why does it have to be my neck? My face was always my best feature, but now no one can see it because of the monstrous fistfuls of skin hanging from my jaw. It isn't fair. If you impregnated that fucking blonde, she'd go the same way, you know? Plus, you aren't a supermodel yourself, you bastard. You and your fucking blonde.*

'There are a million brunettes here, Sam. I meant that woman over there, picking her nose!'

'That is gross!' Sam agreed, congratulating himself for having sidestepped what he could only think of as a dinosaur-sized pile of shit.

'I seriously don't understand. How do some people have such bad manners?'

'Well,' Sam watched the woman have another good dig-around. 'Manners aren't the same everywhere, honey. I heard it's polite to burp after a meal in Afghanistan, or Saudi Arabia or something...'

'That's ridiculous!' his wife sniffed. 'Manners are manners.'

'Right,' Sam agreed, wishing he could have a go at *his* nose. And why not? Why did he have to find a handkerchief? Why did he have to turn away and hide this impulse to shove finger into nostril?

'Of course I'm right. And look, just look! Now she is leaning down to pick something from between her toes! God, people like that shouldn't be allowed out.'

'Aren't you being a little harsh?' Sam asked. Something had obviously fallen on the woman's foot from the cereal counter. If crap fell on Sam's foot, surely the world couldn't expect him to walk around with it till he found a safely private corner and could do as he wanted without upsetting people's contrived sensibilities?

'Sam, we had this discussion before. Sympathy is finite.'

'Of course, dear. But isn't sympathy a good thing? Doesn't it make us better people?'

'Why the hell are you defending her, hmm? You find her attractive, don't you? You must do, since you keep defending her...'

It wasn't out of sympathy for the groaning husband that the mosquito left the couple's table. They simply were not what she was looking for. The common existed everywhere; she wanted something more. Passing buckets of sausages, congealed beans and fruits soaked in thick syrup, she veered towards a queue of carnivores waiting for fluffy waffles.

At the front of the line, Americans armed with fanny packs full of rolled dollar bills and chewing gum waited for their second helpings. Behind them, two British ladies in their prime, their plates painted with bacon grease, stood in what they believed to be the queue for French toast. At the end of the line were a boisterous bunch; a family of Turks. Their fingers glued to the keys of their new phones, they were emailing, texting, facebooking, whatzuping and tweeting mid-conversation, mid-life.

And finally the woman in the middle of the throng. A short, dark-haired Swiss woman with lots of money. She waited in line for a product she couldn't consume, among people who existed in a world she had withdrawn from long ago. She waited, expressionless, as the sweet scent of waffles washed over her straight nose, her perfectly aligned nostrils. She smiled at the simple pleasure as a happy mosquito got drunk on her sugar-drenched blood.

Good morning ladies and gentlemen, this is your master and commander speaking from the bridge. Your Beautiful White Lady has now received the green light from the port authority here in Cotonou. If you are exploring on your own today, you can now proceed to the disembarkation point on deck three. For those of you going on planned shore excursions, please proceed to the Starlight Theatre. I hope you enjoy your day in beautiful Benin. Buon viaggio!

The Rust Bucket

Three passengers of the Grande Mariner walked down the plank, one behind the other. They all wore a green sticker over their breasts with the number 6 written in thick black marker. As they reached the bottom of the piece of wood, covered inelegantly with red carpet, a man in a brown uniform asked to see their ID's.

'They've already checked the bloody card as we left the boat,' Percy Mallory complained as he fished into his breast pocket for the little blue square. 'Do they think we've become different people in the three seconds it took us to walk off the bloody vessel?' His fingers touched upon a gold pocket watch, a small flask and a stubby cigar before finding what they were looking for.

'Are you a police officer?' Chanel asked the man who took her card and held it up to match the photo to her face. He ignored her, which Chanel found very *male,* in a good way.

'Of course he is a police officer,' Percy rolled his eyes behind her. 'Now where is our bus? If they make us wait out here in the heat I will have to write a strongly worded letter.'

'Oh my,' Sister Mary spoke up behind him. Then she was pointing out over his shoulder at the far end of the near empty dock. 'Is that it?'

Ordinarily Percy would have been most irritated with her pointing and the closeness of her hand to his person, but he was distracted by the sight of the rust bucket that might have generously have been called a bus twenty years ago.

'Oh that must be it, look there is someone else from our boat!' Sister Mary breathed before counting off six hail-mary's on her rosary.

'I.D.!' The angry police officer grunted at Percy.

'Now look here…' Percy began looking for a name to fill in the blanks, but the officer's badge which hung carelessly from his thick belt had no name, only a number: 11684.

Ignoring her husband's discomfort, Chanel took

her first step onto Beninian cement.

There are vultures circling overhead. I've counted six of them.

Burt Darwin wrote standing beside the tour bus and the guide, who had introduced himself as Henry.

Our bus is missing a door. It is parked next to the port gates which have been painted in Campbell's-soup-red. Dozens of people are gathered just outside. Their arms are poking through the bars with palms raised. I can't understand their words, but Henry tells me they are saying hello.

'Come on Mr. Burt Darwin. We will go now, yes?' Henry smiled, his white teeth flashing bright against his dark skin. The rest of the company had arrived.

Four passengers boarded the rust bucket and began their journey into Africa. The ride passed without incident for most of the first twenty minutes, not counting the three men who tried to jump into the bus as they pulled out of the dock gates or the flower girl who pretended she had been run over. No, all of that was quite everyday for the streets of Cotonou. It wasn't until they slowed at a red light on the outskirts of the city that a rather unexpected event occurred.

Deep in their own worlds, it took several moments for the passengers of the rust bucket to become aware of the big black man running towards their vehicle with a large cement block. Sister Mary noticed the grimace on the man's face and put her hands together to pray that his pain might ease. Seeing his beautifully toned naked chest, Chanel pressed the zoom button on her camera and clicked away gleefully. Burt Darwin made no interpretation at all of what was going on around him, content with making a note in his journal that there was *a tall man with a cement block*. It was only Percy Mallory that spoke up:

'I say, did anyone notice that fellow charging the bus?'

Their tour guide stuck his head out the open bus door to see, then spoke in rapid Ewe to the stoic driver. The bus lurched forward with sudden speed.

'So we are almost outside Cotonou now,' Henry said quickly, his French accent thicker than ever as he searched through his memory for the correct English words. 'Did any of you notice ze bottles they are selling on ze side of ze road?'

A loud screech came from the back of the bus

where the corner of the cement block struck the license plate.

'Well I never!' exclaimed Percy.

'I did!' Chanel raised her hand. 'Everyone seems to have some!'

'Is it holy water?' Sister Mary wanted to know.

'Holy water?' Burt Darwin looked up.

'I very much doubt that you will find holy water in such an ungodly land, madam,' Percy remarked.

'The bottles are filled with gas,' Henry explained, calmer now that the raging man was out of sight. 'Petrol. You see Benin was having a bad economic times, with bad economy.'

'Preposterous use of the English language,' Percy leaned over to Chanel. She did not care about their guide's language skills. It was the poverty outside that had struck a chord within her and she was furiously taking pictures, trying to capture some part of it. *They have nothing but each other to rely on,* she thought, and sighed with the romance of it all.

'In this bad economy time, gas was very very expensive in Benin, so many people go to Nigeria to buy gas. The gas is cheaper there, and so they bring it back to here and sell it in bottles. Black market,' Henry went on.

'They told me you couldn't buy slaves anymore,' Sister Mary sniffed.

'Why are the children not wearing any clothes?' Chanel wanted to know.

The guide hesitated for one confused moment then shrugged, 'It is hot.'

And it *was*. So hot in fact that even Burt Darwin, who grew up amongst the proper gentlemen of the Low Country, didn't understand how Percival Malory could stand it in his three piece tweed suit. In his journal Burt Darwin wrote:

The English man looks as though he is going to meet his queen. He does not, however, stand out any more than his wife who has chosen to wear a dress that looks like a copy of the one Marilyn Monroe wore when she sang "Happy Birthday" to President Kennedy. Incidentally, "Happy Birthday" was the first song to be sung in outer space. Or at least, the first human song. We are meant to visit a village soon where there will be African singing.

Burt Darwin hesitated, looking out the mud-streaked windows of their bus. Over the years he had found that truth was more true in absence. For that reason, he often observed what he did not observe, which of course could only be based on previous observations.

There is no Starbucks here. No Cafe Nero, no Gloria Jeans, no C & A or Marks and Spencers. There are no drugstores in sight. Walgreens, CVS, Boots are all missing from the uneven pavements. The buildings are all white-ish one-story boxes. Barless windows are rare. I counted five hairdressers on this block and no grocery stores. The shop on the corner has a chicken painted on its wall that looks familiar. Its sign reads: African Fried Chicken.

The bus rolled forward as Burt Darwin wrote, the cheap cement grey giving way to dirt brown. Someday these untamed lands would lie in the shadows of cold glass mountains; big boxes of reflective surface, interconnected windows, energy conscious light bulbs, flat screens and the occasions fish tank. Someday the cheap motorcycle shops and convenience stores would be replaced with sterile apartment blocks with fixed furniture, adaptable to various uses, and stackable. Someday Africa too would be conquered by American rapper culture and Swedish vases, but not today. Today the whities stared out from darkened windows at coconut trees and the dark man wearing a suspicious sign around his neck.

'Such conviction!' Chanel sighed.

'Lord save us!' Sister Mary crossed herself.

'Absolute imbecile,' Percy snorted.

'So true,' Burt Darwin agreed. Having just become a seventh-day adventist, he was certain that the apocalypse would be upon them very soon.

The middle-aged man holding the hastily scribbled sign, on the other hand, did not give much thought to the apocalypse. Osakewe had more immediate concerns.

For ten years now, he had been chasing the skirts of his Josephine. She was, in his esteemed estimation, the most beautiful woman in the world. Skin smooth as waxed coconuts, breasts like watermelons and a body as lithe and delicious as a mayonnaise-filled baguette. She was perfect and Jesus agreed with Osakewe, he was sure of it, which was why He took her into His house. The Bastard.

Josephine was no Nun! She was made for Osakewe. Made to brighten the damp rooms of his small house, made to wash his feet, listen to his woes, and love him – in bed – like a proper woman.

But she had sold herself into church slavery. Jesus worship. What the hell was so amazing about Jesus anyway?

Josephine said her Lord saved the world. Pah! From what? The world didn't feel saved to him. People were dying left and right. Diseases. Wars. Overpriced restaurants with terrible food. Why didn't Jesus save them all from that African Fried Chicken place on Rue Liberté that kept serving people battered rat with a side of food poisoning?

Nah, the world wasn't saved, not by a long shot. They were all living in an unsaved world, a dark place where few lone candles walked – targets for the wicked. Josephine was his candle, he wanted to swallow her light and feel saved. If only for a moment. He would do whatever it took to get her back. If preaching religious babble impressed her, he would preach away.

That's why he was a volunteer now, at the church around the corner from Benoit's Auto-Lotto where he worked. The people at the church were a deluded bunch, but Osakewe didn't mind. He didn't even care that they had him standing here, at the edge of Cotonous' busiest street, wearing a ridiculous sign.

THE END IS NIGH

It wasn't just ridiculous, it was a lie. The end wasn't

coming, it had arrived a long time ago. And the people who still walked the earth? They were all just clinging to the edge of the toilet bowl, like a particularly sticky shit while the deluge fought to wash them away.

The Mad King

Twelve women were dancing in the village square, surrounded by empty plastic chairs. Some shuffled from side to side, waiting for their audience, before unleashing the rhythm which sizzled in their veins. Others had given in to the drums and gyrated like gummy bears dipped in potassium chlorate.

Sweat gathered under yellow and red flower-patterned skirts and coated carved bangles that slipped up and down jerking limbs. The raised brows of Tap, the puckered lips of Swing, the raised chin of Tango, and that ridiculous Jitterbug grin were all absent here. This was no ordinary blending of body and beat.

This was a dance off, African style.

As for the prize for she-with-the-grandest-thrust-of-chest, the quickest-wiggle-of-bottom and the smoothest of everything in between? It was to become the wife of one of the five eligible men that moved amongst the crowd, loitering towards the square.

The whities too, were in the throng. Led by their bored tour guide, their timid steps were out of place with the excitement written on their faces. Westerners always enjoyed the sight of an African's dance. People in the civilized world were too free to let their bodies move freely.

'Blasphemous!' Sister Mary whispered, her eyes drinking in the shifting shapes of arms and legs.

'Brilliant!' Burt Darwin exclaimed.

'Barbaric!' Percy sniffed.

'Beautiful,' Chanel sighed, brushing Henry's arm with her own. 'I wish someone taught me how to dance like that.'

'Real dancing can not be taught, it is revealed from blood,' their tour guide smiled as he pointed them to their chairs.

Percy frowned at the empty seat between himself and his wife. 'You sound like one of those blasted Chinese fortune cookies Chanel keeps leaving around the manor. Ridiculous things.'

'1.35 billion people might disagree,' Burt

Darwin pointed out.

Sister Mary crossed herself.

The head drummer raised his white feather duster, halting the revelry. All faces turned to the man in the black and gold toga that stepped onto the burnt grass of the dance floor. The King had arrived.

'Oba!' Black voices rose as one.

The King inclined his bejeweled head, then moved to the seat between the whities, his face frozen in disdain.

Chanel simpered, her lashes fluttering. A lord was good, but a strong muscular *King* was so much better.

Henry leaned forward, his demeanour respectful for the first time that day.

'Your highness, these are Mr Burt Darwin, Mrs Chanel, Sister Mary and Mr Percy.'

'Lord Percival,' Percy frowned, unimpressed by the village king. 'A Lord of the Great British aristocracy, to be precise.'

The whities were too obtuse to notice the King's expression change. Had the village people been paying attention, they might have seen the signs of anger, the kind often followed by a royal rant.

Alas, they were focused on more important things. The sight of a bouncing breast had possessed the power to dazzle men since the beginning of time – and one of the dancers had lost her top.

The drummers picked up the rhythm.

'Lord Percival?' The King sneered in perfect English. 'Last I checked, Britain was a democracy. That makes your title… just a title.'

Percy blustered and drew himself up to his full height, the top of his head managing to reach the King's chin. 'How dare you insult a member of the British peerage!'

'Oh, I dare, whitey, I dare!' His opponent laughed. 'Why should I hold my tongue when it is you and your ilk that has dragged the world into chaos? Running amok, forcing *Democracy*, an innately corrupt system, on the world as you do… and why? Because of some idiot called Doyle?'

Not one of the whities had a clue what the African was going on about, but that did not stop them from responding. That was the beauty of the fully democratized: not understanding never stopped them from making judgements. A good disciple of Democracy knew little and voted often.

'Your hands can get famous in a Democracy!'

Chanel said earnestly.

'Democracy is no friend of Jesus the King.' Sister Mary crossed herself.

'Democracy is an excellent religion,' Burt Darwin joined in.

'Democracy saved you from the Nazis!' Percy concluded triumphantly.

The King laughed at the white *lord* beside him. 'You forget that Democracy *created* the Nazis.'

Brushing a fly from his right knee, the King surveyed his dancing people, his eyes burning a dark pit of murky brown. 'The human race is base. Most of us are stupid, visionless, unwilling to change. We are full of fear. Fear of the unknown, fear of the stranger, fear of life. Democracy is the rule of the fear-riddled masses. If two democracies don't go to war, it is not because the system is good, it is because its peoples are afraid of death, afraid of change, afraid to stand up to their own corruption. There are no real democracies out there, thank the gods, but even the fake ones stink of rotting intellect.'

As he finished his rant the King went still, his head tilted upwards at an angle to show the white-lord what he considered his best side. There was no need for the Englishman to notice the green-tipped pimple growing on his opposite cheek.

'You're so passionate!' Chanel sighed.

Burt Darwin, who had finished transcribing the speech, had to agree. 'You could start a religion. Although I doubt you will reach a million followers.'

Mary didn't know how a rotting intellect smelled, but she recognized the whiff of blasphemy in the air. She crossed herself quickly and drew a few more crosses over the King and the dancers in the background, just to be safe.

'Utter Poppycock!' Percy panted, having finally managed to get past the lump of indignation in his throat. 'This man is a charlatan who doesn't know the first thing about the world!'

'Oh?' The African King raised a regal brow. 'And what, pray tell, do *you* know of the world?'

'What do I know! What, do I know? I know, that anyone who doesn't extend their eternal gratitude to Britain and her allies for saving the world from Hitler is mad!'

The drums stopped as the angry white man's voice echoed across the village green. The dancers held their breaths. Little ones scampered behind their mothers' skirts. The exposed boob was put back behind wires and elastic. Even the wind paused as History whispered across the African soil: *angry white man equals death*.

'Oh whitey, how ignorant you are.' The King stood slowly, shaking his head. 'You are angry at Nazis for doing *to* the white man, what the white man had been doing to the Arabs of Algeria, the coolies of India, the blacks of Africa for decades.'

Pointing his fat black finger at the balding white head, the King grimaced. 'You, my dear Lord, are *my* Hitler.'

Sinking

'You cannot be serious,' Percy spoke through his nose, his lips pressed tightly into a thin line. He was standing atop a long uneven dock crowded with black men and women in multi-coloured garb. Dead fish lined either side of the cracked pieces of wood, their stench riding little pearls of moisture and popping merrily against his skin.

'You cannot be serious!' Chanel echoed her husband's words as she too caught a glimpse of their boat between the black bodies. 'That thing will surely sink!' Then, having taken in a fish-filled breath, she began to cough.

This called attention to the small group of white people, shiny in the scalding sun. Several locals stopped to stare. They noticed Burt Darwin's shirt and tried to make out what tribe he might hail from. This took up several seconds of consideration before they noticed Chanel.

'Look at the white woman,' a young man said in Ewe.

His companions murmured and clicked their tongues before they all returned to their affairs. To the untrained ears of the whities, this sounded like Xhosa, the African "clicking" language. Of course, it wasn't. The Ewe tribespeople were simply showing their dismay over Chanel's skinny frame.

Their tour guide beckoned for them to follow. 'This way please…'

'Now look here…' Percy began, but he was cut off by Sister Mary who waddled forward, her hands drawing crosses in the air as she blessed the heathen Africans.

'Oh what a lovely contraption! It was a canoe just like this one that saved baby Moses, you know?'

'Wasn't he set afloat in a basket made of bulrushes?' Chanel asked. 'That is *not* a canoe,' Burt Darwin said.

'Moses was a Jew,' Percy said.

'A boat just like this one,' Sister Mary pointed at the pirogue with its bed sheet sail. She took the hand of their tour guide and stepped one foot into the vessel. It shook precariously, sinking under her weight so that its top edges were mere inches above water level. Sister Mary's fingers turned pink in the guide's hand, her lips drawing thin for a split second. She drew a cross with her free hand, and then lowered the rest of her bulk into the boat. Water spilled in from one side and then another, before the vessel steadied itself under her weight.

'The Lord will protect us as he did Moses,' she smiled.

Their guide spoke unintelligible words to a tall half naked boy who was standing nearby with a pole in hand.

The boy gestured angrily. The guide frowned. The boy pointed to the whities and then at the baking sun. The guide sighed.

'Please, take your seats,' he told the remaining three on the dock.

'I'm not getting in that thing,' Percy said.

'I'm not sure,' Chanel swished her fan in front of her face, batting a fly onto the brim of her hat. Her head was beginning to fill with scenes of heroism and romantic rescue. She decided that a near sinking would be just the thing to liven up the day.

'Better than staying here,' Burt Darwin remarked. He lowered himself into the boat beside Sister Mary, holding his journal high above his head. Chanel followed suit and Percy, left with little choice, followed her. Once they were all settled onto their slabs of wood, the top of the boat was almost level with the water.

The tall boy hopped in, followed by the reluctant guide.

Water is sloshing into the boat. Now that the tall boy pushed off the dock with his long stick, the chance to climb back onto dry land has drifted away. The woman, Chanel, is complaining that her shoes are getting wet. She keeps pointing at them and saying "Christian Louboutins", but no one is paying attention. Except Sister Mary who said 'Who are Louboutins? I like them already.'

The guide is now handing out empty water bottles that have been cut into two. He wants us to scoop out the water while the tall boy propels us forward with that stick of his. The boy has no shoes and his little toes sit on-top of his fourth toes. The water is a murky brown, the stench almost unbearable. I understand now why they call this place the Venice of Africa.

'You need to help,' the guide said.

Burt Darwin set his journal on his lap, his look indignant. 'You cannot be serious,' he said. This was quickly becoming a popular phrase amongst the four white tourists in Benin. The other three were quick to agree:

'You can't really expect us to —'

'I mean this is really too —'

'Couldn't we find another boat to —'

The guide tipped his face up from where he was leaning forward to gather bay water in his yellow half-bottle. Regarded from this angle, the strange perpendicular cuts on his cheeks and forehead looked deeper than ever; two grooves on every flat surface of his angular face as if a frightened woman with a great sense of aesthetic equality had clawed him with her sharp nails. His eyes too looked stranger than ever; the whites had turned an egg-yolk yellow.

'Do, or sink,' he said slowly.

A silence settled over the boat. When a black heron flapped its wings and squealed, Sister Mary crossed herself three times. Then one more time, for good measure.

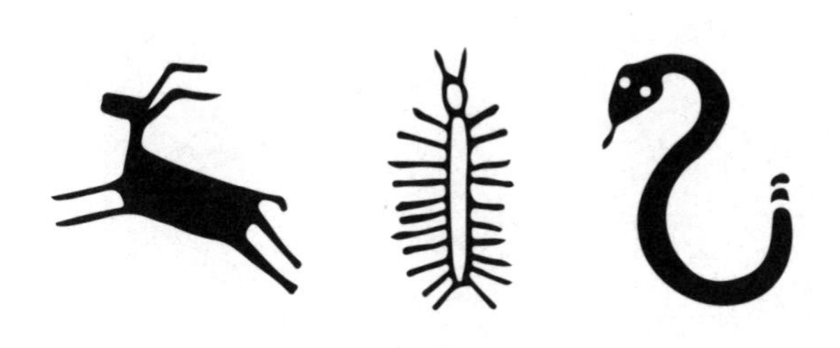

The Venice of Africa

'So, welcome friends to the Lake Nokoue, and to Ganvie, the Venice of Africa.' Their tour guide had recovered from his momentary lapse into the dark side and was back to his jovial smiley-self. 'Ganvie has a population of about 20,000 peoples.'

'People,' Percy corrected. He was feeling particularly contrary since being forced to do manual labour. The only other person who had ever forced him to do work involving physical exertion was his primary school teacher Mrs Leaders who was, of course, fired post-haste. 'And having been to Venice on several occasions I can tell you that this is nothing like it.'

Chanel had to agree with her husband's estimation. The badly-made huts with their thatch roofs were dirty, doorless and built on stilts that looked ready to crumble. A small child wearing a particularly gaudy orange dress with a pink and white squared pattern stuck out her tongue as their boat pushed by. 'Why don't they just live on land?' Chanel asked, distressed.

'They are of the Fon tribe,' the guide said patiently. 'We call them Tofinou – the Water people. Long ago they were chased here by the armies of the Dahome Kingdom. The armies wanted to capture them, and make them slaves. But the Dahome army would not cross water, so the Tofinou built their homes here.'

'Moses was also saved by water,' Sister Mary puffed. She was out of breath from trying to bless the half-bottlefuls of water as they were dumped out of the vessel.

'The Fon?' Chanel said with a laugh.

'Yes,' their guide agreed, to nothing in particular.

Dark brown water sloshed by, a long floating reed skimmed past the tall boy's pole and the sun did its best to boil the bay. Their boat continued on its merry way, somewhere between sinking and floating. As they rounded the corner of yet another group of huts on stilts, the sound of rhythmic drumming filled the air.

'What is that racket?' Percy wanted to know.

It was Burt Darwin who answered with wide eyes. 'Funeral drums.'

'Funeral drums?' Chanel frowned.

'Funeral drums,' Burt Darwin said with certainty.

'Yes,' the guide agreed once more. Sister Mary crossed herself. Their half-naked captain called out to three Africans that stood beyond the window of the hut they were approaching. They rushed out onto the thin platform outside the hut door.

Chanel's eyes softened. They were tall men, all of them, their muscles a glossy ebony.

'This is a craft store,' their tour guide pointed to the hut as they pulled up alongside it. 'We will stop here for fifteen minutes for buy some souvenir.'

'Souvenirs,' Percy corrected irritably. 'And we don't want souvenirs. What else will we see in this godforsaken place?'

'God does not forsake anyone, Mr. Mallory,' said Sister Mary.

'It's Lord, madame.'

'Yes, our Lord.'

Chanel stood slowly and placed her hands into

the outstretched palms of the African's above them. The men helped her up to the hut's entrance, then turned to do the same for Sister Mary.

'Thank you so much, so very kind,' Sister Mary smiled. 'You see Mr. Mallory, you see how helpful they are? Helpfulness is a Christian value. These people are Christian even if they don't know it! Or at least they could become Christian if someone were to help them see the light. Unless they are circumcised of course, then they are beyond redemption.'

'Barbaric,' Percy muttered, clambering up to stand beside his wife. Chanel cocked her head just so, watching the Africans from beneath her large chapeau. Burt Darwin was in mid-air, one foot on the wooden planks, one foot dangling over the sinking boat, his white hands grasped in two black ones, when a woman appeared at the hut door.

The top of her head appeared first, her tight curls poking around the jagged doorframe like hundreds of worms that had learned to levitate. Then came her shiny forehead, her large hooded eyes and her wide, flat nose. When the rest of her body finally made an appearance the whities noticed that she was not really a short woman but she was hunched over so low that her hands dangled a foot bellow her knees and her head was cocked at a quasimodo angle.

Sister Mary crossed herself out of habit.

'Yovo! Wa xo nu!' the old woman grinned. *Whitey, come buy something from me!*

Chanel fluttered her lashes at the still silent black men, then moved towards the hag.

'Chanel!' Percy used his commanding tone.

'Come on Percy, she wants to show us her wares!'

Percy looked around uncertainly, his eyes coming to rest on their guide who had not left the boat. 'Aren't you coming, man?'

The guide shot him a look. 'I will wait for you here,' he said, then returned to scooping water out of the boat.

Burt Darwin and Sister Mary followed Chanel who followed the hag into the hut. Percy stood outside for a moment longer, looking at the five African men around him. The two in the boat were busy trying to keep it afloat, the three standing on either side of him were watching Percy with blank faces.

'Do you speak English?' he said. The men didn't blink.

Disgusted, Percy followed the rest of the group into the dark hut. He didn't see their tongueless smiles as he wandered on.

There was a strange smell inside the hut, a kind of incense that Burt Darwin associated with Asian temples. Long tables made of dark wood lined all corners of the room; they were laden with African goods. Masks, braided bracelets, necklaces, earrings, boxes, black wood carvings of rhinos, elephants, lions, hippos, turtles, frogs and crocodiles. Above the cluttered tables, the old woman had hung scraps of material – some square and some rectangular. They were dyed with bright oranges, reds, yellows, greens and blues and had black ink contour depictions of Africans on them; women carrying water pitchers above their heads, men leaning on their spears, women dancing, men working the fields, women kneeling, men beating on drums, women beating on drums, drums, drums.

'The sound of drums is even louder in here,' Sister Mary remarked as she made a cross over the bracelets she was looking at. No one paid attention to her. Burt Darwin was too busy looking for charms and Chanel was admiring a necklace.

She held it up to Percy, 'Isn't it pretty?'

'Atoon! Atoon do-ll-ar!' the old woman popped her head over Chanel's shoulder, grinning her toothless smile.

'Eve axi din!' Chanel said quickly. *That's expensive!*

The old woman cackled with glee. 'Ah ! Yovo se Fongbel!' *Whitey speaks Fon!*

'A little,' Chanel agreed. The few sentences she knew were courtesy of a romance novel she had read a while back featuring an African princess of the Fon tribe who was captured by a dashing English pirate. 'Do you know Princess Tata?'

The old woman cackled and reached out for Chanel's hand. 'I know much. I will tell you all. Atoon do-ll-ar!'

Percy's nostrils flared. 'Let go of my wife, Madame!'

'Is she a fortune teller?' Burt Darwin drew close. Sister Mary was right behind him, painting crosses in the air. The junk lying about was forgotten as the old woman knelt quickly, surprising them all with her agility.

She held up her hand and thumped the ground. 'Atoon do-ll-ar!'

'Atoon to you Madame, what utter tosh!' Percy took a step towards the door.

'Oh come on Percy, there's no harm in a little bit of soothsaying.' Chanel smiled prettily at her husband as she handed a five dollar bill to the hag on the floor.

The eerie cackling filled the room once more, followed by a string of words no one understood. The money disappeared underneath the colourful collar of the wild eyed African and then she was rocking back and forth, humming a strange tune to the rhythm of the funeral drums.

Her eyes rolled back, then closed firmly shut. Her shoulders swinging, backwards and forwards, the floorboards creaking, creaking, creaking. She was muttering now, muttering and murmuring quickly. Suddenly her hands began to rise, shaking her whole body, shaking, and then she was screaming. Yelling loud and shrill.

And then it was silent. The old woman was still. One eye popped open. She cackled.

'That's not funny!' Sister Mary protested as her fingers loosened their death grip on her rosary. Chanel and Burt Darwin were not amused either and their expressions said so.

'I'm starting to find this one amusing,' Percy remarked over the old woman's continued hilarity.

When the room was once again silent except for the funeral drums, the Fon woman pointed at Chanel. 'You. Stay away from Sun. Run from it, or you will die.' She turned her gaze to Burt Darwin and to him she said in the same bored tone of voice, 'You have a spirit following you. Find two centipedes, dig a hole, cover it up and never look back.'

Centipedes? That's rich ain't it, Burty-boy?

That is all the woman said. Then she was on her feet again, as quickly as she had knelt to the ground and she was holding up a necklace.

'You like? I make you good price!'

Made in China

'I think it's pretty, non?' Chanel insisted as she held up the colourful necklace to the scorching sun.

Sister Mary tossed out another half bottle of water before looking up. 'Our Lord would not be pleased with your consumerist ways.'

Chanel shot the woman a scathing glance. 'My Lord is most pleased that I have helped the African economy. These people are starving, you know!'

The boat swung abruptly under Sister Mary's affected shock. She held her hand to her breast, her rosary swinging from her fingers, her mouth gaping like a fish. A rather dim-witted fish.

'Well I never!' she said at last, dredging up the three words from the pits of her much-layered belly.

Percy muttered unintelligible words, their tour

guide pretended he couldn't understand and their boat boy actually did *not* understand.

Off to their left, two skinny boys and a girl with short hair looked up. They were floating amongst a field of golden reeds, trying desperately to set up their fishing net just so, But the sight of the shiny white people took precedence over all else. They stared unblinking at Sister Mary, taking in her large ankles and thick wrists, drinking in the layers of her neck fat. By the time the white people's boat sailed out of sight, all three children were full.

Burt Darwin spoke next. 'I doubt it was made here.'

'What do you mean?' Chanel was frowning.

'Those coloured stones look more like plastic,' Burt Darwin explained. 'A classic Chinese look really.'

'Chinese?' Chanel held the necklace close to her face, thumbing through the black beads and running her hands over the long orange, red and yellow stones amongst them. 'But they are heavy, like stones!'

Burt Darwin would have laughed at the innocence of the woman if his mama hadn't instilled in him the importance of manners. In South Carolina, out on the houseboat where he grew up, the distance between their home and their neighbours had never been more than a foot or two. The harbour was a crowded place, and the houseboats always got shoved to one side when the cargo ships rolled in. And despite all that, it was rare for neighbours to piss on each other's boats while relieving themselves in the mornings. And that, his mother always said, *is cuz us folk have them manners.*

So Burt Darwin didn't laugh at Chanel. Instead he reached for the necklace, his oily moustache twitching as he considered. 'I'd bet a bucket of crispy fried chicken skins that's made in China and these here rocks are full of sand.'

Percy frowned. The whities watched as two women and their babies drifted by on a slab of woven wood. Sister Mary crossed herself. The only relevant action was taken by Chanel, who searched inside her bottomless bag until she pulled out a nail file, a bottle of silver nail polish and finally a very pointy pair of nail scissors.

'Give it to me.' She took the necklace back and pierced the stone with the tip of one blade. The sand that streamed out of the hole spilled across Chanel's soaking shoes and into the puddle at the bottom of the boat.

'I've been had,' Chanel said, and in her surprise she dropped her French accent. In that moment she sounded very much like an actress in one of those Hollywood movies where the native language of the Nazis is broken English laced with a tinge of Germanic staccato. Indeed, if she were dressed in an SS uniform instead of a Marilyn Monroe classic, who for all her blonde hair was too fond of James Joyce and gypsies to be a Nazi, Chanel may well have been playing one of those parts. None of the other passengers took note of her momentary lapse. They were too busy watching a long slithering creature strike out and swallow the necklace which Chanel had dropped overboard in disgust.

'Was that what I think it was?' Sister Mary said, breaking the silence that had descended upon the group.

'How on earth are we meant to know what you're thinking?' Percy complained. He bent to fill his half-bottle with boat-water with more vigour than ever.

'Today is Thursday,' their guide said. 'The day of Damballa's preference.'

'Damballa?' Burt Darwin perked up, smelling the supernatural in the air. 'Is that a voodoo God?'

'Not God,' Henry said. The marks on his cheeks squished together and disappeared with the horizontal stretch of his mouth. 'He is a L'wha. An intermediary to Bondye the Creator.'

'You are talking cobblers, sir,' Percy said.

'L-wh-ah,' Henry repeated, then laughed from the depths of his belly.

Sister Mary crossed herself.

'Right right,' Burt Darwin rolled his hand in the air. 'But what does Damballa do?'

'Do?' the guide looked confused. 'He is an ancient L'wha!' This time, when he said L-wh-ah a small drop of spit landed on his brightly coloured pants. 'He is a member of the house of Rada! He is the guardian of our morals!'

Chanel snorted, unimpressed by the sort of God who guarded morals. Percy was not listening anymore. Sister Mary crossed herself.

'You pray to him so that he guards your morals?' Burt Darwin asked, hoping he had misunderstood. In his mind only gods that could gain you points in the afterlife were worth worshipping, and this Damballa character was turning out to be sadly worthless.

'No, we feed him hardboiled eggs so that he

guards our morals' Henry said. 'He prefers them when they are presented on mounds of flour.'

'Jesus would not approve of you serving hardboiled eggs to blasphemous snakes,' Sister Mary announced with grave severity. 'Any more than he would approve of rollerblades. Dangerous things rollerblades, very dangerous.'

'Oh, we are saved!' Chanel pointed at the fish dock up ahead. She was once again playing Rose. Now, if only Damballa would tip the boat over and drown the others, everything would be right in her world.

Some Bad Luck

Dead bits of fish cooked slowly in the puddles under the docks as the tourist bus rattled away in a northerly direction. The mud tracks that led from Ganvie to Ouidah had no potholes whatsoever. Potholes only developed on roads where man had tried, with cement and other dreamed up mixtures, to flatten a stretch of ground. No such activity had taken place in this part of the country. But while there were no potholes to be found, there certainly were bumps.

All sorts of things got caught and compressed under the ancient tyres of the tourist bus. Sometimes they were not significant enough to be felt by the whities who travelled over them; flowers, little rocks and leaves were among such things as were beads, beetles and discarded cola caps. But on some occasions the tires would crunch over black cocoa nuts, termite hills and green mambas and on those occasions the bus would rattle, as it did at the very moment Burt Darwin opened his diary excitedly.

I just saw a snake fall from a tree. Its head slipped in through the open window above Miss Chanel's head, but was quickly pulled down to the road by the weight of its body. I think we might have driven over it just now.

Burt Darwin was right, except for one thing. The mamba had not *fallen* from the tree. The green snakes had developed a hunting method several decades ago: dive onto the moving vehicle, slip through the open windows and bite the offending humans. It worked for many a snake, but this one had run into some bad luck.

Chanel reached up towards the cobweb-covered air-conditioning vent above her seat, her fingers almost touching the dry tufts of spider silk before an itch on her nose had her pulling her hand back. With one long nail scratching along the hawkish curve of her nose, she took note of the men driving their motorcycles in the opposite direction.

'Where are all the motorcyclists going?' she asked, peeved. None of them were noticing her. Not a single accident had been caused by her stunning beauty, which was unacceptable really. Chanel decided that the fault lay with the dirty windows that made her appear black from the outside. 'You should get someone to clean these windows.'

'Quite right,' Percy agreed beside her. 'They barely let the light through! How am I meant to read the paper in these atrocious conditions?' He rattled that morning's cruise line paper angrily.

Burt Darwin scribbled in his notebook while a drop of drool arched down the corner of Sister Mary's chin; she had been snoring since they splattered the snake.

'Those men are working like taxis,' Henry said, addressing Chanel's question, his dark face revealing nothing of his thoughts. 'It is like I said before: We have bad economic times. The old president threw out all foreigners long ago then we have the bad economy…'

'It's *your* people they threw out,' Percy said to his wife. 'The French were terrible at being a colonial power. No one could ever throw out the British, our empire reached the farthest coasts in the world...'

'Of course dear,' Chanel answered.

'You must read about the empire,' Percy went on. 'The sun never set on it! And we invented everything that is of any use. The steam engine, the telephone, penicillin...'

'Didn't the Scots invent those?' Burt Darwin asked.

Percy went slightly blue but was prevented from responding to this great insolence when Sister Mary stood abruptly.

'Jesus, Mary, Joseph, the Holy Ghost and all the Angels!' Her voice got louder as she pronounced each name, but it could not be described as a fully-fledged yell until the moment that she pointed out the window. 'THAT IS OUR WHEEL!'

And so it was that for the next four seconds the four tourists and their tour guide watched as their tyre rolled with great speed, passing them at first and then knocking into a palm tree. On the fifth second the bus simply clonked down onto where the right back wheel used to be, temporarily knocking the air from the passengers lungs.

'You cannot be serious!' Percy brushed at the cultivated creases of his tweed suit. Chanel's fingers rushed to her costly breasts as if to make sure the impact had not knocked the silicone out of them. Sister Mary crossed herself and Burt Darwin opened his journal, flipping to a fresh page.

We are stranded in Africa

It didn't take long for Henry to usher the whities out of the broken down tripod, calming them with his glow-in-the-dark smile.

'It is no need to worry. This is authentic African experience you pay for. Now, here we are standing on the very road where slaves walked.'

Chanel, who had been about to voice a complaint, fell silent. There was a certain romantic quality in their predicament. The image of a chiselled Ottoman Sultan and women wearing silks and chains filled her mind. She clapped excitedly.

'Was it right here?' she asked, rubbing the rough road with the slick bottom of her shoes.

'Oh yes,' Henry nodded, then putting his hand around her shoulder he turned her to face a two-storey building hidden behind leaning palm trees. 'That was the house of Francisco de Souza. In his garden the slaves are sold and then they walk on this road to the Zoma-i.'

Chanel flushed, wiggling in the strong African's

grasp like a captive.

'What is the Zoma-i?' Burt Darwin wanted to know. He was hoping it was another Voodoo L'Wha, but one that could gain him points for the afterlife.

'Is anyone at all concerned that our only means of transport has just died a miserable death?' Percy asked.

'Yes, many slaves died on this road,' Henry agreed. 'Many did not want to be slaves so they swallowed rocks or tried to drown in the lagoon over there.' He turned and spoke in rapid Ewe towards the skinny shadow of their driver, before walking on. 'Follow me please, we will see more of beautiful Benin and *real* Africa while the driver fixes the bus.'

The path was dusty and quiet except for the sporadic shrieks of fruit bats. They flew from one palm tree to the next, looking for shade to dangle beneath. When Chanel's sharp heel caught in what appeared to be a spider hole, Burt Darwin flipped open his journal of truth.

Heavy clouds are gathering overhead. Sister Mary's fringe is stuck to her large forehead. A few yards to our left is the lagoon where Henry says slaves tried to drown themselves. It is surrounded by marshland. Henry says we aren't too far from the beach where the slaves were put on boats, 10,000 at a time. 10,000 on one boat, how many bathrooms did they have?

'My Louboutins!' Chanel held up the broken heel for all to see. Burt Darwin put on his "oh pity" face, but none of the others took note of her trembling lower lip. She was not very good at crying on the spot. She was better at being the impassioned slave who fell in love with her master but would not give into him unless he married her. 'I am a survivor!' she cried out. Then raising her chin in the air, her defiant eyes on Henry, she took off her second shoe and broke the heel off with deliberate slowness.

Henry watched her with understanding. He had played master in many women's lives. His mistress knelt before him often as did his wife's sister. Only his wife, the misbegotten spawn of Damballa, would not give him the attention that was his due as king of the household.

'Your wife's violent tendencies are positively unChristian,' Sister Mary told Percy, not bothering to lower her voice.

'Madam, we Christians have often found need

to resort to violence to spread the good word,' Percy said, his fingers patting his jacket over his breast. 'Just think of the Crusades.'

Not knowing what to make of that, Sister Mary resorted to drawing a cross in the air. 'You did not tell us who Zoma-i is,' Burt Darwin complained.

'Not who,' Henry smiled his Cheshire-cat smile. 'The Zoma-i is the place where light does not go.'

Where Light Does Not Go

Sister Mary had managed to live out the first fifteen years of her life without ever breaking a sweat. She might have experienced the discomfort of a wet patch beneath the armpit if she had played sports or been an excitable child or lived anywhere other than Juneau, Alaska, but she had not. The first drop of water-chloride-urea mixture that pushed through Sister Mary's skin had appeared under her left nostril just as Samuel Smitherton leaned forward to kiss her. Though Samuel left Juneau the very next day (he was on a day-tour with a cruise ship and sailed away back to California) Sister Mary's new relationship with sweat continued. She perspired her way through high school, half a history degree, a marriage, a divorce, a gambling problem, a stint in jail and an excommunication from the Catholic Church. Now, under the heat of the African sun, Sister Mary's sweat dripped in a steady flow; down the dark little hairs of her moustache, the thin little hairs on her nape and the prickly little hairs in the place where light did not go.

'This is where the Zoma-i used to be,' Henry indicated vaguely towards the empty marshland. 'It was a big room with no windows. The slaves were taken from the market to the room to sit in the darkness.'

'Why?' Chanel's tragedy sensors were tingling. She was imagining herself in the dark room with all the other slaves. Big strapping young black men...

'To lose themselves,' Henry shrugged, as if it should have been obvious. In the darkness, where bodies were distinguishable only by breath, where slaves sat for weeks at a time their eyes growing useless, heavy... the fight left even the strongest people in such places.

'The poor souls!' Sister Mary sighed, then bending she plucked three small red berries off a spiky leafed bush. 'When are we going to have lunch?' she asked, chewing a mouthful of pink pulp.

'I could do with something myself,' Percy agreed.

Henry watched Sister Mary chew, then shrugging again, he led on. The whities would have their authentic Africa tour.

'Many slaves died in the Zoma-i…' Henry flashed his teeth at Chanel as they walked side by side ahead of the others. Sister Mary followed close behind, keeping pace with Henry's shadow as she blessed the countryside with pink-stained fingers. Percy paid little attention to what was happening around him. He walked an equal distance between Sister Mary and Burt Darwin as he muttered about the heat, the lack of newspapers and the indecency of a country that did not serve tea and scones.

Dust is rising around us, a strange yellow orange colour. The soil is powdery, drier than the baby talc I used on the heat pimples in the crease between my ass and legs. It is itching. My ass I mean.

Burt Darwin looked up from his squiggles. It was he who noticed the tree first, even though he was bringing up the rear.

The tree loomed tall over the countryside its roots had weaved their way in and out of the soil, its branches reaching up and out like a Geisha's fan.

'Look,' Chanel pointed her perfect silver polished finger ahead. 'It looks like Alice's tree!'

'Who on earth is Alice?' Percy frowned.

Chanel clicked away on her camera. She had always wanted to be the Queen of Hearts. 'Oh and we've followed the Black Slaves Road to get here, it's just perfect!' She continued to click away on her camera as she hummed, 'Follow the bla-ack slave road. Follow the bla-ack slave road. Follow follow follow follow, follow the bla-ack slave road...'

The others had stopped listening to Chanel a while back, so no one noticed that she had mixed up her fairytales.

'This is the Tree of Forgetting,' Henry said solemnly. Henry was a more convincing liar when he was solemn. 'I would advise you to stay away from it, look if you must, but from here.'

'Why?' Burt Darwin wanted to know.

'Yes why?' Chanel echoed the question.

Henry's eyes narrowed. 'The slaves who survived the Zoma-i were brought here to circle this tree. The men nine times, the women seven and then poof!' He clapped his hands together, 'Just like that they would forget who they were!'

It was then that Sister Mary took off at a run,

her chubby ankles flashing under her shapeless skirts. 'Hello tree!' she giggled as she half-crashed into and half-hugged the ancient bark. 'It's so big!' With her arms tight around the trunk and her chest crushing the large black ants that quickly reformed their northward line to travel around this new obstruction, Sister Mary leaned back so that she was looking back at the group.

'I bless this tree! I bless it in the name of the father, the son and the holy ghost!'

'Sister Mary?' Chanel called out.

Sister Mary is now skipping around the Tree of Forgetting. No matter how many times Henry asks her to, she refuses to stop. Chanel seems quite upset. She has been digging in her bag for something, though I don't know what. She told her husband that shrill laughter makes her feel ill. Lord Mallory does not seem to care, one way or another, but he did say, 'My God, the woman is foxed!' Sister Mary is singing the "ring-a-ring-a-roses" song. Henry is looking displeased. I'm hungry and my butt still itches.

'Sister Mary?' Henry tried to calm the woman that was now sitting at the foot of the tree, her eyes shut as she continued to laugh.

Percy ran out of patience and marched up to

the guide. 'This is preposterous behavior, sir, and that you are allowing it on your tour is beyond comprehension!'

'Oh, look! Someone is coming!' Sister Mary smiled as she pointed out towards the road.

'That is Mr. Burt Darwin as you well know, Madam!' Percy spoke with disgust.

'Mr. Darwin?' Sister Mary frowned. 'The heretic?'

The whole group gathered around the tree, watching as the middle-aged woman blinked her confusion. 'Who are you people and where is Tom?'

Thomas Cooker is Rotting in Hell

It didn't take long for Burt Darwin to realize that the Sister Mary they knew was no longer with them. This woman's name was simply Mary and all she was interested in was one Mr. Thomas Cooker, a.k.a. Tom.

As far as Burt Darwin could gather, Tom was Mary's ex-husband who had received the death penalty from the State of Oklahoma some eighteen years ago. Mary didn't mention under what charge, she just kept repeating: 'Oklahoma fried him good!' and 'Where's my Tom?'

Burt Darwin fingered the talismans around his neck, bringing each one up to his eye. *Hell. Hell. Hell. Purgatory. Hell.* Yes, the overwhelming consensus seemed to be that Mr. Thomas Cooker was in Hell. Unless of course he was crawling around in someone's bathroom as a cockroach. In Burt Darwin's mind the cockroach scenario was just as likely; he was not a man who picked favorites among religions practiced by over one-hundred-million people. As for religions with less than one-hundred-million followers, for them Burt Darwin employed a very complex system:

- For any religion with more than fifty-million followers, Burt Darwin would reserve thirty-minutes of his day. This half hour would be spent in practice of said religion, whether it be through reading of a holy scripture, chanting, praying or a simple verbal acknowledgment of the faith.
- For religions with one through forty-nine million followers, Burt Darwin dedicated ten minutes each.
- Any religion with less than a million followers was beneath his notice

He relied on the ever-reliable Wikipedia for these figures.

At the very moment when Burt Darwin converted from Shintoism to Cao Dai, Henry made a very serious announcement.

'Stop!'

This exclamation provoked a surprising array of reactions among the whities.

Chanel, who had convinced herself that the handsome black tour guide and she were going to begin an affair shortly, believed that the outburst was indicative of a fit of conscience. She was both right and wrong, as it happened. The affair would take place, but Henry had no conscience to speak of.

Burt Darwin, who was reciting the Kinh Thiên Dao, the prayers of the Heavenly and the Earthly Way, thought perhaps the time for being Caodaist was over, and checked his watch.

Mary let go of the grass she was about to shovel in her mouth and Percy snorted:

'Stop? We are not moving. We should be moving! Where is that damned bus?'

'I mean, we must go back,' Henry spoke slowly, as if to a group of young school children. In Henry's experience, children who went to school suffered from the same sad stupidity as these whities.

Something about school seemed to slow the brain. His own bastards had no such problems. At age eleven and sixteen, they were both making a living off their wits. 'We must take Sister Mary to see a Healer.'

'Who?' Chanel asked. She had given her hat to a rather hot looking Percy, and was busily pinning a stray hair back into place.

'It is obvious that she is suffering from an ailment of spirit,' Henry explained as he patted Mary on the head. 'Do you see that glazed look in her eye? And those huge ankles! The Healer will know what to do.'

'Her ankles *are* huge,' Chanel agreed. Mary didn't seem to care that four pairs of eyes were now taking in the swollen masses of skin above her ugly sandals.

'Then I will require a rooster,' Burt Darwin interjected after making a quick note in his journal that *Ms Mary is chewing on grass.* He knew that traveling into the spirit world was not an endeavor to be taken lightly. It did not matter that the Healer would do the travelling, being present was enough to put one in harm's way. The only thing for it was to hide behind a rooster's soul; they made humans invisible to evil spirits.

Burty-Boy, you don't really believe that, do you?

'Why do you need a cock?' Henry looked

puzzled, but he needn't have bothered with the question as Percy was having none of it.

'No one will be requiring the services of livestock today, thank you!' Pulling out a folded bit of paper from the inside of his jacket pocket, Percy held it a few inches from his perspiring forehead. 'Aha! Just as I suspected. No Shaman on the description of the tour. In fact, this tour is also specified as requiring "light walking", a matter which I will take up with the cruise director the minute we are back on the ship. No, no, we have lost enough time already! We are going to the Temple of Pythons and that is all there is to it.'

'But Percy,' Chanel looked towards the woman under the tree who was busily smelling her own armpits. 'Isn't she sick? I mean, those ankles!'

'Sick?' Percy arched an unimpressed brow at his wife. 'Up until a few moments ago, that woman was a *Catholic*. That, my dear, is a *true* condition.'

'I need food,' said Mary, standing suddenly and looking around the group. 'My Tom doesn't like skinny women. Where can I get some food?'

'See? She's talking more sense already!' Percy smiled. 'Now lead on Henry, surely there will be something to eat at the temple.'

Bat Woman

After a little consideration and weighing of the money to be made from a visit to the witch doctor with the loss of tip from Lord Percy, Henry realized he was faced with a no-brainer. Leading his flock around the moat, he circled back to a village on the outskirts of Ouidah, and asked for directions to the nearest Vodun priest.

'This is the python temple?' Percy asked, suspiciously as they approached a mudbrick hut with colorful murals. Above the door, a large mermaid holding a snake had been painted in brown, blue and white.

Henry ignored the British man, calling out to the resident of the establishment.

Henry has brought us to another village, this one

bigger than that of the mad King. Huts are strewn across the dry soil. A strange-looking lizard just ran past my left foot. It had a yellow head, rye body and orange tail. Ms Mary saw it too and tried to step on it.

A woman has come out of the hut we are standing in front of. She is wearing only a long white skirt and lots of jewelry. There are dozens of colorful necklaces across her chest and armbands and bracelets. Some are made of shells, others look like plastic. Each of her fingers is adorned with a large silver ring and she has white paint across her forehead and lips.

'We are sorry to intrude, but this woman needs help.' Henry flung one of Chanel's hands from his arm to pull Mary forward.

The priestess did not move.

'This is outrageous!' Percy's face turned a now familiar tomato red. 'After I specifically told you no more straying from the plan!'

Henry shrugged off the much shorter man's excitement, resuming his chat with the African woman, this time in Ewe: 'Yo, Nani?'

'He is so assertive!' Chanel remarked, oblivious to her husband's growing fury.

When the priestess, having shaken hands with Henry, peered into her face, Mary smiled, 'You are pretty.'

'What I am is a Priestess, consecrated by the goddess Mami Wata!' the woman replied, pointing long white acrylic nails at the mermaid painting above her door. 'Come, we will ask what problem you have.'

Mary followed the pretty woman happily, once again chewing on already soggy strands of hair.

Burt Darwin uncapped his pen, ignoring the voice that whispered in his ear:

Did you get a look at them titties ol' boy? Mmmm mmm.

Percy too, followed the priestess into the makeshift temple. Having decided not to tip Henry after this blatant disregard for the schedule, he was cheered by the prospect of keeping the 10 dollars he had been prepared to part with.

It was Chanel that refused to enter. There was nothing romantic about playing second fiddle to a topless woman.

'Henry, I don't feel so good. Maybe you can walk with me a while?' she simpered. The only way to combat breasts was with breasts. Everyone knew that.

The inside of the mud hut is covered with paintings of the same mermaid goddess, Mami Wata. There are candles in all four corners. A short wooden figure smoking a cigarette is standing on a mound of what looks like flour. The priestess says it has great power.

'Apologies, Madame, but my wife seems to have lost her way…'

'Stop!' the priestess pointed to Percy and then the spot beside the smoking-mini-man. 'You and your friend sit there.'

'How dare you — ' the Englishman used his favorite phrase, but the look levelled on him by the priestess stopped him cold.

'Sit.'

It is hard to say what made Percival Mallory, Lord of Staffordshire, in the green and verdant land of England in the glorious Great British Empire, obey the half-naked African. If he hadn't, there is a chance that he may have come across his wife and their tour guide fornicating amongst the trees behind the small temple. While the sight would not have changed the outcome of this particular story's plot, it is hard to say what kind of *feelings* it might have produced. The author would guess next to none, but then the author is rarely right.

'All of this is my wife's fault,' Percy muttered.

'Sorry?' Burt Darwin frowned. He wondered if Ms Chanel had powers he had been unaware of.

'She chose this bloody cruise. Who in their right mind travels to the heart of darkness?'

Interesting question, Burty boy. Do you know anyone who is in their right mind?

'I could be having high tea at Cliveden House and instead I am sitting on the *ground* in some witches' mudhouse.'

Yes, he must be crazy. Why don't you offer him that ring of yours? Maybe he'll have the guts to do what you haven't been able to in years.

'She is a priestess, not a witch. Her power comes from that fetish behind us,' Burt Darwin told the English Lord, twisting the ring around his finger before returning to his notebook.

The priestess has placed two small silver balls and a cowrie on the ground. Now she is removing two of her necklaces. One is covered in what looks like dried seeds. The other has little bits of silver with some kind of imprint on them. She threw them on the ground. Now she is leaning over the pile on the floor. Lord Percy is not looking at the woman. He keeps casting sideways glances at the smoking-mini-man.

'Nuvavieusom!' the priestess announced a moment later. 'She must eat the wings of a bat and she will remember.' Then, grabbing a green bottle, she sprayed Mary with the liquid inside before walking out of the hut and leaving three confused whities behind.

Half-an-hour later, the group from the Grande Mariner were walking back to where their bus was to meet them, two bat wings richer and $108 poorer. The money had been handed over by Chanel against the protests of her husband.

Henry led the band of misfits and his unsatisfactory lover trailing behind him in broken heals. Mary lumbered a few paces behind the Marilyn Monroe dress, chewing on a dried bat wing as she watched the sky. Burt Darwin and Percy brought the rear, deep in conversation.

As Percy spoke in hushed tones, Burt Darwin was watching Mary. While in Trinidad, he had come across a native who told him that if he drank the blood of bats, he could become invisible. A Tyrolean gypsy in Austria had claimed that one had to carry the left eyeball of a bat to accomplish the feat. In Oklahoma, you had to carry the right eyeball (pierced with a brass pin) and in Brazil it was a bat's heart…

Burt Darwin's eyes narrowed, wondering when Mary would disappear from their sight.

And then she did.

To the surprise of all, except Burt Darwin, Mary made a break for it. She ran. Quicker than anyone would have thought possible, she crossed the dead earth and crashed into the edges of the rare west African forests like a water buffalo. She skipped over thick tree roots and foot-long centipedes, swallowed two flies and scared small creatures half to death before Henry caught her, in the semi-darkness, beneath the canopy of leaves.

No one else had followed the woman, and Henry believed that the others had been too afraid of the darkness to dare. This reaffirmed his belief in his superiority and made him smile despite having been led on a merry chase.

What Henry didn't realize was that the whities back on the road were not afraid of the dark. They were far more afraid of light, of exposure and of the unidentified creepy crawlies that were trying valiantly to recover from the shock of Mary's single-woman-stampede.

The Wishing Tree

Two school children stood on the side of the road, their bare toes showered in orange dust in the wake of the bus that carried the whities across Africa. The boy, the older of the two, grimaced as he caught the skinny white woman at the back window of the vehicle pointing her camera his way.

He was used to tourists and their fascination with photos. At first Samuel hadn't minded being their African momento. He quite liked the idea that his reflection was being carried to far off places. His face would be looking out from photo albums onto foreign living rooms. People he didn't know, people who had no effect on him whatsoever, would be watched by his image. He was intruding into their lives. He was entering their eyes. He was burying deep inside their minds, becoming a part of their memories… The whities, they thought they were taking something from him, but he was the powerful one.

So at first, he had liked having his picture taken by the… what was that word that white woman from UNICEF taught him? Ah yes, con-de-scending. Those con-descending bastards. Then Nora had pointed out that just one of their cameras could pay for an entire year's worth of food and clothing for *both* their families.

And that pissed him off.

He turned to Nora now, noticing the way her hair hung in a large braid over her left breast. Sometimes he felt she was smarter than him. That made him angry too.

'You are strong,' Nora said suddenly.

'What?'

She tilted her head towards the disappearing bus that was had left them standing as the only representatives of the human race on that stretch of road.

'The whities with their hollow cheeks and stick-limbs. In a fight, you could kill them all with your bare hands.'

Nora was smarter than her classmate could possibly have guessed. She read the likes of Achebe and carved poetry into the river bank when she took her father's goats for their baths.

She was also right about the whities. Even at 12 years old, Samuel was stronger than all of the tourists, and Percy was by far the easiest mark.

Lord Percival Ambrose Mallory checked his pocket watch for the seventh time since leaving the slave route. It was not because he wanted to know the hour; he had taken note of that the first time he plucked the gold-plated object out of his breast pocket. Neither was it due to a fondness for the object, left to him by his useless brother who had had the audacity to die at the age of 67 in the arms of a rather ugly prostitute. No, Percy was not a sentimental man and his memory, as well as his sense of time, were spot on.

He had no problem recalling, for example, the first time he had tried chicken tikka masala at his high-school sweetheart Jessica's winter cottage. He had known then that foreign foods were not for him. Jessica turned out not to be for him either when, the day before he was going to propose, she announced that she had gotten engaged to his father. James John George Mallory the Earl of Durham was a bastard through and through, but not enough of one to marry his youngest son's girlfriend. Oh no, it was all a demonstration of will. The Earl wanted his son to marry into a connected family; a dentist's daughter would not do for the Mallorys.

Percy also had no problem recalling the sweet sense of joy he felt when he found out his brother was shooting blanks. Percy could not have thwarted the Earl's dream of coddling grandchildren without the happy coincidence, not when his brother was so bloody keen on having a couple of wailing poo machines of his own.

Not giving his father the joy of grandchildren was not punishment enough of course, so Percy had spent the entirety of the Earl's life making sure the man was miserable. The Earl wanted his sons to be politically driven; Percy got himself and his brother caught by the paparazzi on a particularly iffy outing involving men, women and livestock. The Earl wanted his sons to be well educated; Percy switched to a double major in creative writing and art history at Cambridge. The Earl wanted him to marry well; Percy proposed to a hand-model.

Oh no, Percy's memory was spot on. What was *not* spot on was that Mary woman and her infernal jabbering. So, not having access to pen and paper, Percy was showing his displeasure by the only means left to him. The restless and repetitive movement of pulling out his watch and putting it back in his pocket would, in his estimation, irritate his fellow passengers and signal to them his displeasure. And Percy *was* displeased. He would have been even more displeased had he realized no amount of clock gazing would penetrate the drowsy haze that had enveloped the rest of the passengers of the once-again-four-wheeled rust bucket.

In fact, everyone but Percy was asleep by the time the as-yet-faceless driver rammed the breaks, bringing the bus to a halt.

'Wh-at!?'

'How dare you — '

'Thomas?'

The whities composed themselves while trying to place where exactly they were. Burt Darwin wiped drool from the corner of his mouth, and pulled out his pen.

We have stopped in front of a brown arched door surrounded by a low cement wall. There are vendors about with stalls full of fruits and baskets of mayonnaise filled baguettes. The driver is standing at the front of the bus beside Henry. His nose is flared and there are vertical cuts on his forehead and cheeks. He is taller than Henry. Uglier. His bloodshot eyes are watching Ms Chanel although she is too busy fixing her hair to notice.

She has pretty hair.

'Finally! Now where is that infernal Temple? Let's see the bloody thing and get back to the ship, I do not wish to be in a rush to get changed for tea.' Percy stood, sounding none too pleased.

'Of course,' Henry stepped back, his broad shoulders brushing the drivers as the Africans allowed the English Lord to descend into the swarm of opportunists who had gathered at the entrance of the bus.

Chanel left her camera on her seat, the diamond on her finger sparkling as she reached out for Percy's arm.

Burt Darwin stepped off the bus next, peering at each vendor with interest. Bananas, coconuts, wood carvings, bracelets and a couple of water color paintings of the wooden door and its surrounding walls. His disappointment was evident in the droop of his moustache.

'Bonjour Madame, Bonjour!' A boney man latched onto Mary's sweaty arm just as she descended the stairs. His eyes, alive in a body that had begun decomposing many moons ago, gleamed as he lowered his voice. 'Come. I will sell you *power.*'

'Power?' Mary blinked. Neurons fired across her damp scalp, lighting up memories that had been gathering cobwebs under the reign of the holy Sister.

Her father standing beside her as she squeezed her right index finger against the trigger of her first shot gun.

The loud thump when the deer went down.

Her fingers tight around the hunting knife, slicing between skin and bone.

Her foot slamming against the gas pedal of her old truck and she headed South.

Thomas asking her to dinner after fixing her car's overheated carburetor. Thomas telling her he loved her.

Ticking the green box at the abortion clinic.

Staring calmly down the barrel of Thomas Cooker's gun.

'I have power,' Mary said, moving to follow the others through the wooden door.

'This is the wishing tree. Worshippers of this temple make a wish here and if this wish comes true, they need to come back and sacrifice a small animal to the Gods.' Henry explained as he stood in front of what appeared to be a particularly gnarly tree. He watched the pale faces carefully for their reactions. This was his first tour with white tourists, but he knew instinctively that *this* was what they had really come to see.

Blood.

His flock stepped closer as he finished his little speech, their eyes searching for tell-tale marks of it. They wanted blood.

'What if their wish does not come true?' Chanel wanted to know. A small yellow spider crawled across the brim of her massive hat as she reached out to touch the accordion-like bark.

Henry shrugged, 'Then the Gods have not willed it.'

'How convenient,' Percy snorted.

Burt Darwin finished his inspection of the branches with a frown. 'I don't believe many wishes have been granted recently.' To him that spoke volumes about the influence of these particular Gods. He was not impressed.

'Jesus, Mary and Joseph!'

It appeared that some part of Sister Mary was still present in the woman who pointed a very large finger towards the clearing just beyond the wishing tree where lots of dead things lay.

Where Dead Things Lie

As Burt Darwin stared down at the mangled carcasses on the mud floor of the Temple courtyard, it dawned on him that his career as an artist had always been doomed for failure. The fact of the matter was: art was dead.

It had died at the very moment of its birth. There was no way to explain what *was,* no way to re-tell it. No moment, no feeling, no scent, nothing that *was* could be recorded with any accuracy – not even in his mind. His memories were faulty, his senses limited, even the notes he took in his journal of truth were his truths only because like art, Truth was nonexistent.

He looked at the s-shaped curves the blood had made as it seeped out of one of baby goats' throats.

He had painted in similar shapes while studying at Savannah College of Art and Design. His teachers had hailed him as a genius then. While his classmates emulated their personal heroes, obsessing over subject matter or *saying* something meaningful, Burt Darwin had let his brush guide him.

Right, left, up, down, circles, squares, curving S's… the less his paintings said, the more people saw meaning in them. For six years he sold every canvas he made at his gallery in Ellis Square. And then, just like that, it was over. His fingers were tired of painting the meaningless. They wanted to create Truth.

But Death was the only Truth he could find. And Death could not be recreated; it either was or was not.

Thus it was that Burt Darwin pinned his hopes on the afterlife; a place where he believed a real Truth might exist. He became obsessed with the possible "other sides", studied Holy texts as he had once studied Van Gogh's brush strokes, Klimts palette and Vermeer's rendering of natural illumination.

While Death became more and more certain with every piece of information gleaned, the afterlife became more unfocused. Just *any* afterlife wouldn't do. He needed one where he would continue existing as himself, free to observe the Truth he longed to uncover. He would also prefer the Afterlife to have stretched canvas, paints and Oreo's – he had always painted his best work after gorging himself on the black-and-white mini-sandwiches. Yes, cookies, paints, a few brushes, some canvas and Universal Truth were all he required from the place he was going. His needs were few, easy to satisfy and many an Afterlife would do him. The problem was which one to aim for.

So Burt Darwin had decided to solve his dilemma by following the advice of one Rene Descartes and believe what the masses believed; just in case.

Opening his journal, Burt Darwin put his pen to paper, ignoring the anguished cries of his fingers.

There are six dead baby goats on the floor. Their throats have been slit and their bodies dragged across the mud. Eight men dressed in white cloth are sitting on the other side of the courtyard, drinking out of halved coconut shells and watching Ms Chanel who has bloodied her pretty white dress while hugging one of the carcasses to her chest. Lord Percy looks angry. Mary is laughing and Henry is trying to see what I am writing.

'Mr Darwin, that notebook… are you a writer?'

'No.' Burt Darwin shut his journal, frowning at the invasion of his privacy. 'Writers worship words. I only practice religions with a million or more followers who worship entities that can provide in the afterlife.'

'Pardon me, but are you planning on doing something about this!?' Percy wheezed, his small eyes moving between Henry and his wailing wife.

'What you want me to do?' The tour guide asked. 'If she wants to be with the dead, she may.'

Percy was about to remind the impertinent African that crying and dead livestock were not on the tour description when, Chanel stood up. She had noticed the blood on her hands and had decided to play a far more fulfilling role than the upset animal-lover.

'Out, damned spot!' she muttered, rubbing her hands together as she rejoined the group of whities.

'Silly woman,' Percy huffed, then followed Henry's pointing finger to the round cement hut on the other side of the courtyard. 'You would think she would practice restraint. Has to be that surrender-monkey heritage. Those Frenchies just have no sense.'

'Nonsense my Lord, nonsense!' Chanel said,

following Henry across the bloodied mud.

'Perfect sense,' Mary agreed, laughing as she skipped behind them. 'It all makes perfect sense!'

'What makes sense?' Burt Darwin looked back, stopping just in front of the hut door.

'Everything,' Chanel smiled taking her husband's arm. 'Except. Well, who would have thought the little goat would have had so much blood in him?'

Frustrated by the sheer stupidity of his fellow travellers and even more so by the lack of adherence to their tour schedule, Percy shook Chanel's hand off his arm, stomped ahead through the hut door and walked straight into the pit of pythons.

Snakes and Ladders

Sometimes humans just got on his nerves. There he was, minding his business, slithering here and there, not even complaining that he hadn't been graced with legs or arms, trying really hard not to be grumpy about the cramped living conditions in this bloody place and what did he get in return?

That's right. A giant ass on his face.

No. He was willing to put up with the occasional grabby hands, the being slung round shoulders and even the endless chanting of his worshippers but enough was enough. A couple of rats and some hard-boiled eggs served on mounds of tasteless flour would only go so far in placating him! This guy was just plain *rude.*

He had to be taught a lesson. Of course, chances

were he wouldn't *learn* his lesson. If seven years of being prayed to had taught him anything, it was that humans weren't the sharpest tools in the animal kingdom. There was that one woman for example... what was her name? Francine something or another? She had been coming to him for three years now and it was always the same damned request.

Stop my husband from cheating.

First off, if you want your husband to stop cheating, why don't you wash your hair from time to time? Ugh, how he hated her long stringy hair. Kept brushing along his skin, giving him the creeps. And secondly, why are you asking for such a stupid thing? Monogamy made no sense, any animal worth its salt knew that.

So what if some dumb-ass birds mate for life. And then there were those gibbons (total retards), wolves (freaky bastards) and some weirdo termites. Well congrats. A few bizarre creatures who are monogamous mainly because they don't know better or are freaked about infanticide and humans figured, hell yeah, *that* must be the natural order of things.

Seriously, that Francine chick could learn a lot from him. How did *he* go about mating? Simple. When it was time, he just went for it. Found the nearest snake, licked some pheromones off its skin to make sure it was female, et voila! Ba-da-bing, ba-da-boom, job done. None of this, what's your name, do you like me, oh no don't go mate with the next guy crap.

But that was neither here nor there. He was in the mood to digest some expensive Italian shoes and he was a male, and a God, so he'd damn well do as he pleased!

'Bloody Hell!' Percy's squeal bounced off the domed hut, startling all 83 pythons surrounding him in the pit. Well, all except for the one who had his left foot and part of his calf in his mouth. 'Get it off me!'

Hearing the commotion, the tourists, Henry and several of the worshippers filed in through the narrow doorway, spreading out over the thin circular platform above the deep pit in the center of the room.

'Oh God, is he dead?' Chanel turned her face into Henry's shoulder, trying not to notice the aroma of onions wafting from her African's armpits.

'Of course he isn't dead, it'll take hours for the acid in the snake's body to burn through Lord Percy's trousers and then many many more for his skin to begin melting,' Burt Darwin informed the group.

'Have you all gone mad? Get me out of here!' Percy screamed, watching the snake's head inch upwards towards his knee.

'Was Kurtz mad?' Chanel asked suddenly.

If anyone had been listening, they wouldn't have known what she was talking about. As it was, however, no one was listening.

Burt Darwin was trying to decide if saving a human life would get him points for the afterlife, or if standing against nature was a No-No.

Mary was remembering how Tom's head had banged against the back of the electric chair until the very last moment of his life. Death by snake, in her estimation, was a much nicer way to go.

Henry was debating if a death at the Python Temple would make the place more or less attractive to the average whitey travelling to Africa.

The worshippers had no qualms about the ugly bald man dying. One of their Gods had chosen him as food and that was perfectly fine. On the other hand, they had a mandatory donation system, which visitors only paid as they left the temple…

Grabbing the rope ladder that was propped

behind the hut door, two worshippers jumped into the pit of pythons.

A moment later, Percy screamed.

41 Virgins

If Percy was honest with himself he would have acknowledged that the reason he was going along with yet another unscheduled stop in what was turning out to be the world's worst shore excursion (in his distinguished opinion), was that he was still shaken by the sudden fashion with which a stranger in a white toga had stabbed the python who was attempting to swallow his leg… in the head.

If Mary were honest with herself she would acknowledge her slight or maybe even not-so-slight disappointment in not being able to watch a fellow human bested by a footless, armless, wordless creature one tenth his size.

And if this author were honest, she would acknowledge being tempted to make Percy python food for the sheer fun of it.

'The deluded may doubt the power of this sacred forest,' said Henry sweeping his hand in long zigzags across the air and swatting a black fly, followed by a flying beetle and Chanel's bloodied dress. 'This is the place where King Kpasse came to escape his enemies and where the gods turned him into this tree.'

'How romantic.'

'Utter tosh.'

'Hmm.' Mary stepped over several fist-sized centipedes to take a closer look at the ancient tree at the center of the clearing just beyond the forest gates. It looked old. It was big. But if it were not for the antelope-horned statue with the massive penis erected beside it, it would never have drawn her attention. 'Who is this?'

'He is Legba.' Henry smirked, watching Chanel gazing at the statue. 'The gatekeeper of towns, villages and houses.'

'He looks like he should be a God of fertility,' Mary remarked.

'He looks like the devil,' Chanel whispered, entranced.

'What about the others?' Burt Darwin asked,

opening his journal. Seven statues surrounded the big tree and Legba, all standing in an imperfect circle around the transformed King.

Shango is the God of rain, lightning and justice.

Sakpatassi is the God of small pox.

Aidohwedo is the God of rainbows, continuity and wealth.

Houeda-Dangbessi is the God of Pythons.

Ogou is the God of iron.

Heviosso is the God of thunder.

The last one in the circle is Tohossou, the God of deformed children. Henry says because of Tohossou, deformed children were worshipped in Ouidah while in the North of the country they were considered to be witches and killed. Mary went a little pale when she heard that. She is still fanning herself.

People are coming through the gate. They are all dressed in white robes. Henry looks surprised. He is walking towards the old woman who is leading the large group. It looks like there are 45 of them plus the rooster in the old woman's hands.

'Why does she have a rooster?' Burt Darwin asked with a worried tone. He was a practicing Anglican at that moment, and was not keen on the idea of being privy to devil worship.

Henry rushed back to the whities who were all staring at the approaching crowd. 'We are very very lucky!'

'What are you going on about, man?' Percy frowned.

'It is the priestess. She is here to cleanse the town. She has brought 41 virgins for the ceremony.' Henry spoke as if his flock should have known that.

'Are they going to get rid of these centipedes then?' Mary shook one off the toe of her shoe, then grimaced when Burt Darwin scooped it up in his hat.

'I need one more.' He looked around, unable to choose from the multicolored bugs scattered across the ground.

'Ew, I stepped on one!' Chanel squealed, then shot one of the prettier virgins a withering glance.

Bald spot gleaming under the African sun, Burt Darwin plucked the half squished creature from beside Chanel's foot and headed in to the thick of the forest leaving all the virgins and non-virgins, beasts and killers behind.

Do you really think you can get rid of me that easily?

His amulets jingling, Burt Darwin moved forward with great purpose.

We have been together for 14 years Burty boy. Remember the time before you started pretending that you can't hear me? You tried a million different things to get rid of me back then, didn't you? Salt circles...holy water... you even brought in an exorcist. Well, he called himself an exorcist, but I think we both know he was drama major from the community college close to your aunt's house. I like your aunt, by the way. She's hot. When are we going back to see her?

Burt Darwin checked his watch. Islam time. A new page had been uploaded to Wikipedia a few days ago: "Islamic Prayers to Ward off Spirits". He had spent hours memorizing them:

'E-uuu-zuuu bi vej-i-la-'

Oh come on man, more arabic mumbo jumbo? At least take me back to the virgins. 41 virgins, freakin' hilarious. Do you think they really are virgins? I doubt it. I mean, who is these days?

'Kelima-ti-la-til-'

A couple of those girls were seriously hot. Did you notice how tall these West Africans are? The legs just seem to keep going and going...

Finding a shaded spot under a bat infested tree, Burt Darwin bent down, reciting the prayer as he dug his fingers into the mud. In the distance, drums began to play, and the whooping sounds of the dancers could be heard.

Ow. What the hell was that? Hey, you! Stop that! I'm talking to you. Why don't you stop being a dick for the first time in years and actually talk to me?

Having made a hole the depth of a kidney-bean-tin, Burt Darwin plunked the half dead and the wriggly centipedes into the pit and sat back. There were only two lines left to the prayer.

'Spirit, tell me one thing before you go...'

You are kidding me. It's Kenny. I told you a million times, it's Kenny "the dog" Brown. You know that. We used to talk, remember? Back before you went to that retarded shrink that messed with your head...

Burt Darwin clenched and unclenched his fists. 'You're about to leave for good, *spirit*, but before you do, I want to know. What is it like?'

What is what like?

'The afterlife! Is there Truth where you are?' Burt Darwin asked, his eyes scanning the emptiness around him.

Man, you are about to exc-or-size me and you want info bout the afterlife? You gotta be kidding me if you think I'm gonna tell you shit.

'You owe me, *Kenny.* You've been stuck to me ever since my niece and nephew used that damned Ouija board thingy in my house. You owe me and you know it!'

Kenny was quiet for a while. Then, there was a palpable shift in the air followed by a strange popping noise and a very faint: **fuck youuuuuuu.**

'Bastard!' Burt Darwin stared at the half-dead centipede rolling at the bottom of the hole. The healthy one must have managed to crawl out, because it was gone. Just like his spirit. Kenny had let go. The little bastard had severed the tie he had been cultivating for decades and floated away.

Retrieving his hat, Burt Darwin retraced his steps through the forest, continuing to recite prayers. It was only when he reached the clearing that he noticed the silence.

And the dead body.

Cold Sandwiches

Five women sat on plastic chairs, chatting with lowered voices as they munched on mayonnaise-filled baguettes. They were a privileged few. Not everyone could have their lunch in the mortuary.

Eating a sandwich in one of the only truly cold rooms in the city was an honor bestowed upon the wives of connected men. The pathologist's wife was usually amongst the ranks of the privileged, but today was an exception. Today, Jacques Burribeau did not allow his wife to join him in the cold room. When the police chief, who even now stood beside him, told Jacques of the dead white woman, he knew he did not want his wife looking over his shoulder on this particular day. Dead white people were a rarity on his table, and he didn't want anyone sending him withering glances because he may have looked at a certain body part over-long.

'It is the strangest thing, Jacques. When we arrived on the scene, there she was lying in the midst of a cleansing ceremony, dead. No sign of struggle. No blood. I interviewed everyone of course, but they all say the same thing: she was dancing with the dancer wearing the sun mask and then she just collapsed!'

Jacques was half-listening to the detective as he inspected the woman's legs. They were long, thin and so very, very white.

'I mean, it could just be that she was sick. I mean, look how skinny she is!' The detective continued, a look of distaste on his face. 'Why are you trying to unbutton her dress man, just cut the thing off!'

Releasing the buttons on the back of the white material, Jacques let the body shift back down and frowned. He had wanted to keep the dress. His mistress was a good seamstress, she would have been able to make use of it.

'That's it, cut, cut, cut. The bloody ship's captain asked me four times already if there was any "foul play." What a ridiculous expression. "Foul play". I told him, sir, this is no *play*. A woman is dead.'

The police chief's laughter surprised some of the ladies into looking towards the table. Jacques flicked his wrist, his snarl making them turn away quickly. He was not averse to allowing the women to sit in his room, but they were not allowed to look at the bodies. Looking was *his* privilege. Removing the last piece of material, he gazed at the size zero in front of him.

'Say, what is that weird smell?' The police chief sniffed, lowering his nose towards the woman's head.

'Please chief, you will inhale toxic gases,' Jacques stepped forward quickly, waving the policeman away. The chance of the chief recognizing the smell of bitter almonds as the scent of cyanide was slim, but slim was chance enough. Jacques was not going to give the white man his money back if the chief blew the whistle on this autopsy and called it a murder.

'Right. Of course.'

'To be honest chief, this is looking like a classic case of malnutrition. This woman is extremely underweight. Electrolyte imbalance, Ketoacidosis...the number of problems caused by malnutrition that lead to cardiac arrest are too numerous to count. I would say that this was most certainly a heart attack. '

The police chief scratched his head, then reached into his back pocket. 'Does malnutrition cause mental problems, too?'

Jacques wasn't sure where that question had come from, but if it was going to appease the police man he'd agree. 'Yes, of course.'

'Then this is starting to make more sense.' The chief waved a folded bit of paper at the body, 'I found this on the body on the way here. It was pinned to the inside of her skirt.'

'What does it say?' Jacques asked, although what he really wanted to know was what the policeman had been doing under the dead woman's skirt.

Unfolding the bit of paper, the policeman cleared his throat:

Kara Chanel,

We were doomed, fratino, from the womb. Mama was proud when we taught ourselves to read and write at twenty-six months and five days. She laughed when Uncle Johannes brought us a 1000-piece puzzle for our fourth birthday and we had it done before Papa could bring out the Einstein cake. And when we finished school at twelve, do you remember that party Mama had? All the neighbours came, everyone drinking like it was Purim. Then Mama did like her drinking. She always quoted Esther: drink till you do not know the difference between 'cursed is Haman' and 'blessed is Mordechai'. A strange story that. We always wondered how we were meant to see the King as good, when he was so pleased to see Haman swing from those fifty-foot gallows. Could anyone who is appeased by the death, any death at all, be good?

But that is an obsolete question now. Now that we know the truth about Good and Evil.

I don't really blame Mama for not predicting the course of our life. For a chosen one, she wasn't very bright. And that is her fortune. That, and the silver backed brush she smashed across Papa's face when he said he was leaving her for Frau Patzval from the grocery store.

He left us too, I know. And it hurt you, I know. Feeling your pain has always anchored me to this world. Well it used to anyway.

Mi ne scias. Mi ne scias, Chanel. Was there anything I could have done to prevent this? Maybe we shouldn't have studied epistemology, linguistics, maths. Maybe there was an area of knowledge that can disguise the truth of the world. Mi ne scias.

Either way, it is too late for me. But not too late for you, fratino. You have to spread the true word. You have to tell people that it is not safe to study. Not studying is best. A stupid, gullible and naive population drowning in humanitarian ideals and philosophy with little or no grasp of reality is healthiest. Such a person is healthiest. Whether through culture, religion or a severely crippled school system, the world must spread the unintelligible belief in happiness and love as key ideals. We must discourage the spread of Nietzsche and his ilk, and give knighthoods to Romance writers. Royals and celebrities too must be applauded for keeping the masses on track and all forms of Acting – in particular the Stanislavsky method whereby the individual lives in a constant state of hand-picked emotions – should be applauded. Sports, and the watching of sports and other such bizarre fascinations for basic physical co-ordination are not to be belittled – not only do these activities dull the mind, they are also an outlet for violent urges and great wasters of time.

Above all, we must never forget the importance of manners. Without this arbitrary set of behavioural regulations the truth of human nature will be revealed and we will return once again to an age where man did not pretend to be superior to animals and was content to be exactly what he was: a beast whose life is brutish, short and solitary.

My dearest Chanel, never forget that you are doing the right thing. Remember what you learned during your years in Den Hague. Right and Wrong exist only where there is lack of information. Too much information colours the world grey. Pretense is the only way forward. The habit of imitating is congenital to all humans from birth, the pleasure that is taken from it as real as anything can be. Pretend and help others to do the same.

Those who help open others eyes to Truth are doing humanity a disservice. A day will come when they too, ignoble creatures, will die and their deaths will only be tragic in the eyes of those who pretend.

Kara Chanel, my fratino, mein schatz. Forget me, mi perdigis, but never forget you are doing the right thing.

Via vico.

Ursula

Silence reigned in the cold room. The women had stopped chewing to listen, their sandwiches going limp in their hands as they tried to pick up on the few words of English they understood. No one moved.

'Kara, fratino, King whats-his-name, what does any of it mean?' the policeman scratched his head, looking over the strange markings on the paper in his hand. He was not an ill-educated man, and while he didn't recognize the universal language of Esperanto (which was not really all that universal) he did notice how the handwriting on the page seemed to change slowly through the sentences. From small cramped letters to sprawling cursive, it looked as though two different people had written on the page.

The pathologist leaned over, casting a suspicious glance towards the sandwich eaters who had resumed their activities, before making a show of trying to decipher the words. 'This is not even written in a real language!' he declared after a moment. 'She was obviously mad.'

'Yes. She was obviously mad,' the police chief sighed.

'Hey don't look so down, chief. This is cause for celebration!' Jacques patted Chanel's cold thigh twice before covering her with a sheet. 'The dementia, the lack of fat… this is an obvious case of cardiac failure. We can all go home now.'

An Englishwoman and an Alleged Scotswoman Argue over Binoculars

'Isn't it just so appropriate?'

'Isn't what just so appropriate?'

'Well that blonde hand model dying here, of all places!'

'Muriel, what on earth are you going on about?'

'Oh, for heaven's sake, Caroline. We are in *Contonou!* Didn't you read the cruise paper this morning? It means *Mouth Of The River Death.'*

'It does?'

'Didn't I just say so? Oh, oh, look, that must be the hearse! I figured they would take her body on board.'

'How'd you figure that?'

'Well, they can hardly leave her in Africa now, can they?'

'They must have graveyards here, too. I don't understand why they would bother taking a corpse all that distance. She is long gone after all.'

'I guess her husband doesn't agree. Did you see him earlier on the Lido deck? He was having a cup of tea and biscuits, or maybe it was a scone – either way, he didn't look that upset to me. Of course he is a Lord, so he'll probably have a new wife lined up before we reach London.'

'He looks pretty upset to me…'

'How can you tell? I can barely make his face out from this distance. I wish our room was on a lower floor, it's almost impossible to see the dock from here!'

'You wish no such thing, Muriel. I've watched you ask almost everyone we've met what deck their room is on. Do you think they don't realize that you ask only so you can say ours is on the penthouse floor?'

'My dear, people are idiots, of course they don't realize. Anyway, none of those fabulously envious looks are worth missing out on what is going on down there at this moment! Oh, if I could only see who that is now, standing beside Lord Mallory!'

'That's the captain of course, and it looks like some policeman on the other side of him, and someone else… Ah look, here comes the coffin.'

'How are you seeing all of that? My eyesight is much better than yours, which is only natural since I am nine-months younger… excuse me, what did you just hide behind your back!?'

'Let go, Muriel!'

'Binoculars! Ah, Caroline, sometimes you are truly a genius!'

'Just have your look, then give them back. I want to see if Lord Mallory cries.'

'English people don't cry. It's drummed out of us in the cradle. In fact, I'm pretty sure there is very little that is considered ruder than subjecting others to a physical demonstration of grief.'

'You think crying is *rude?*'

'You wouldn't understand, Caroline. You're Scottish.'

'I was born and raised in London!'

'So? Your mother is Scottish, and you think all the colourful paper they print up there is actually legal tender. *That* says it all.'

'You know Muriel, you can be a real—'

'Oh, how strange…'

'What now?'

'That is hardly an appropriate response to my earlier statement.'

'What?'

'There you go again. Single words that are meant to stand for entire sentences, it's vulgar. Must be the Scottish in you…'

'It is efficient, so stop being a hag and tell me what is strange!'

'Are you using the word hag in its middle English or Scottish definition?'

'What!?'

'Are you calling me an ugly old woman or a *soft place on a moor*? Hard for me to say since you are Scottish…'

'Sometimes I wonder how I stay sane with you constantly yammering in my ear.'

'Sanity is a matter of perspective, dear. As is strangeness, and *that* is certainly strange.'

'What are you pointing at? Oh just give me the darned binoculars!'

'Calm yourself, Caroline! Grabbing is the height of vulgarity. Unforgivable really. I'm pretty sure my father, God rest his soul, once said "those who grab should be shot." Or was it murdered?'

'Muriel, you are really trying my patience…'

'Oh, come now. It is Lord Percival, he is speaking to a red-nosed man with very ugly stringy hair. Here, have a look.'

'Finally. Oh. That is Mr Darwin. I met him a few nights ago at the Casino just off of Cape Town. He was a bit odd…'

'Odd? Odd is interesting. Go on.'

'He was playing the slot machine beside me and asked the waitress for water.'

'Water at a casino?'

'Yes, that is what I wondered about too. So I listened into the rest of their conversation and I have to say, he has a lovely accent. Something very Rhett Butler.'

'Southern accents are quite pleasing. They make one think of good manners.'

'They do.'

'Unlike the Scottish accent…'

'Which I don't have…'

'Thank God, that would have been tragic. So, what did he say?'

'I can't remember his exact words of course, but

he said something about his fingers itching and that he was trying to strike it rich for the afterlife.'

'Well, it looks like he might have struck it rich after all!'

'How'd you mean?'

'It's what I found strange earlier! I could have sworn I saw Lord Percival give Mr Darwin something rather glittery and yellow.'

'You don't mean—'

'The "Eye of the Tiger." Exactly!'

'But, why?'

'Who knows, Muriel? Who knows?'

The two women on the balcony of room 1999 were distracted by the sudden shrill cry that came from below. A woman in Mother Teresa clothing was wailing as she ran out of the ship and onto the ramp where four African police officers were carrying Chanel Mallory's thin coffin. Unintelligible yelling about fortune tellers and suns was followed by the large woman knocking into a completely unconnected tourist who was trying to get back onto the ship. The unconnected tourist, one Edward Schmetterling, lost his balance and fell into the murky waters of the port of Benin.

It was because of this fall that Edward would

miss a phone call from his wife who was calling him from their home in Washington, D.C. The missed call would confirm in her mind (and rightly so) that he was not in fact on a work retreat, and was having an affair. This in turn would lead her to hit their stash of Christmas booze and forget to pick up their teenage son from soccer practice. Their son, Mark Schmetterling, would then decide to walk the three miles home during which he would J-walk in a quiet residential area. Distracted by a passing crow, a woman in her late 30's would almost run Mark over. Her nerves shattered by what might have been, she would call her ex-husband in a fit of tears. Her ex-husband would listen to the voice message from the love of his life six times, then decide not to press the red button under his fingers.

Had he pressed the button, a nuclear missile would have launched from the rogue American submarine swimming off the shores of Cape Verde and killed several million people in Moscow, which would, naturally, have led to Russian retaliation, which would have prompted the Americans to declare war, which would have made the Chinese join the fun, the Iranians to say "me too!" and tada, WWIII would have been upon us exactly 16 days, 18 hours, 9 minutes and 52 seconds from the moment right before Sister Mary knocked a Schmetterling overboard.

And so, as much as this author may want you to feel fear and pity, pity and fear at the sad end of Dr Ursula Krietmeir, B.A., MSc, PhD, the fact remains that the death of Lady Chanel Mallory saved the world.

Epilogue

The Beautiful White Lady was busiest when the large clock in her Atrium struck six and the doors to the grand dining room were opened for early seating. The passengers filed in, two by two, feet following walking sticks, following walkers, following a particularly short waiter who pointed the way with white gloves.

The chandeliers swinging above the gathered masses were level with the closed second floor and one large shadow. Capitano Stefano Alighieri surveyed his passengers with a peculiar expression. Those who chanced to look up would see a man in his early 40's. Clean shaven. Slicked-back hair. Dark bushy eyebrows. Right eye black, left eye for some reason blue. A pressed white uniform, its gold epaulets four striped with a half nelson denoting his superiority to all others on the ship.

If someone chanced to look up, that is what they would see. Their master and commander. But few ever did.

The Captain shifted his weight, scratched his leg and narrowed his blue eye. The kleptomaniac was at work again, her clever hands sneaking jewelry off necks and wallets out of jackets. She weaved round women with long dresses until she was beside a fat, pedophile. He would have loved it if she dipped her little fingers in his pocket. Small hands were as good as it would get for him in this childless place.

The blue eye skimmed over nymphos, schizos, psychos and people with bum-chins to the man who was currently Muslim.

'Captain?' the rasp of Veronique, the ships most expensive escort, reached him as Muslim-Darwin poured salt into his right palm and licked.

'Very few people know that particular teaching of Muhammed.'

'Sorry?' Veronique simpered. She was frightened. The captains lip curled – he sucked it in. Her fear tasted of sugared dates.

'Come over here, piccola troietta.' He beckoned with his hands, the gold embossed cufflinks catching chandelier light. The redhead did as she was told, her mid length hair brushing the creamy expanse of her strapless shoulders. 'See that man? The one in the Brioni suit.'

Her fear wiped out by the mention of the exclusive suit makers, Veronique nodded. 'Lord Mallory. I read up on him, but he is here with a blonde – a very young blonde.'

'Not anymore.' The Captain smiled. No other letters were necessary. The escort went forth to woo and eventually rob the unwitting Percival.

Satisfied, the Captain returned his attentions to Darwin who had pushed his steak away in favour of a pale coq au vin. His notebook wasn't on his person. Uncharacteristic, the Captain thought, his blue eye seeing everything. The patches of sweat under Darwin's arms. The new wrinkle on his forehead. The missing ring.

There was something about rings, the Captain mused. There had always been something about rings. Gyges and his invisibility ring. Eleazar with his demon ring. Solomon's ring. Wagners ring. Merlin's ring. Kingmoor's ring. The Ring of Dispel, the Ring of Mudarra and of course the Eye of the Tiger.

The Captain let loose a short laugh.

Mankind's obsession with circles was so wonderfully primitive and so very fitting. The circle ruled the world, after all. Leaning one tanned hand on the gold balustrade he adjusted his tie pin with two longish nails.

The black eye rested on an old woman in a red blouse gripping the arm of a blonde in her thirties. 'Abused daughter becomes abusive mother.'

The black eye rested on a man with a greasy mustache and red nose. 'Addict owns drug, drug owns addict.'

The black eye rested on a woman in nun's garb. 'Woman gets mad, madness gets woman.'

The black eye narrowed on Darwin. The Captain smirked. 'Egg becomes man who eats egg and wonders which came first, when there are no firsts. Egg-man looks for straight truth, when everything straight lies. All truth is crooked. Circular. Life, like a sandglass, is always reversed and runs out, again and again. Zarathustra will always come down the mountain. Darwin will always go on his voyage. And arrive. And discover. And forget. In the ring of death and life. For a ring. Over. And over. Its finished. Almost finished. Never finished. There is only the voyage.'

The Atrium clock stuck 6:30. The blue eye blinked. The ding-dong-chimes announced the imminent arrival of his voice. The room went silent as the Captain reached for the small silver microphone in his pocket.

Good evening ladies and gentlemen, this is your master and commander speaking from the bridge. I hope you are all enjoying your dinner, while your Beautiful White Lady makes its way out of the Gulf of Guinea. Tomorrow we have a Sea day, so do remember to visit the Narcissus Spa for a well-deserved massage and don't forget to check the cruise paper for the many fantastic activities the crew have planned for you. The skies were a bit overcast earlier, but we have emerged to gaze upon the stars again, so relax and enjoy as your Beautiful White Lady takes you on the journey of a lifetime. Goodnight.

Acknowledgements

I'd like to thank Adrian Searle (who is to blame for publishing this novel), Rodge Glass (who edited all the way to page 42 before writing in the margin: "*umm isn't this a bit racist?*") and Blythe Robertson (who took Burt Darwin for lunch, but still owes me a birthday meal. That's right. I remember.) Cheers. Thank you. Merci.